I0541358

# The Sirens

# The Sirens

# Stavros Stavros

The Artless Dodges Press

*The Sirens*
*By Stavros Stavros*
ISBN 0981993915
EAN-13 9780981993911
*© 2009 Artless Dodges, Inc.*
*Published by The Artless Dodges Press*
*Cleveland, Ohio.*

*Cover design and other illustrations by T. Maven*

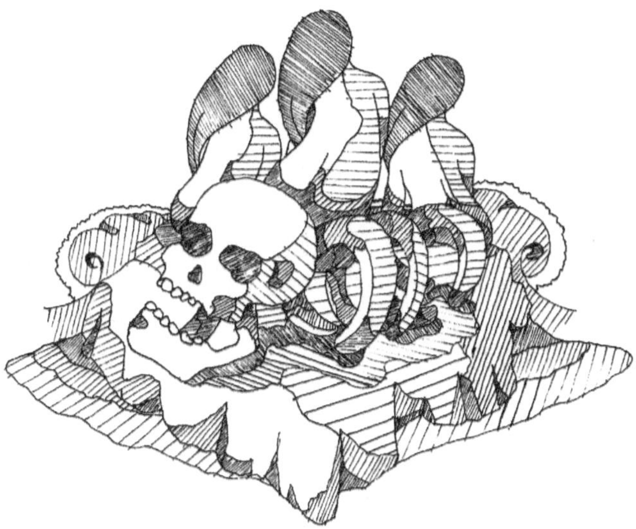

# CANTO ONE § DESIDERATUM

# 1

Where did these characters - this absurd *ensemble* - begin?

It is not so simple a question! I am tempted to say only that they arose from an idea, a fragmented thought, a passing sentiment! Yet that will hardly suffice, for what is the origin of the idea? And what mind could be that produced it? Perhaps the question can be simply satisfied with the explanation that they began with a man standing beneath a window, behind which a girl was singing… Where does any art begin? A thousand trivialities congeal and, in their arrangement, reveal something more: I saw a man standing beneath a window, I saw a girl singing; there is within me what I have called Artist, and he remembers! (And yet there is Devil there as well: and Savior, Absurd Man, Child…!)

Yes: naturally I cannot speak to their origin without drudging up with it certain pertinent aspects of my own; nor would I want to! Indeed, the sole purpose of this review is that lingering hope that I might infer more of myself, might come to know more of myself, might yet unlock that confusion into which I am plunged! The lingering hope that by discerning the nature of that sensibility whose workings produced these meager offerings (you laugh: I have exalted them as Art, yet now declare them meager!) I might understand this madness; that the compulsion producing these strange and horrific events owes its conception to those years! That I might yet shed light upon the fragmented whole to which my parents assigned one name, the ever-embattled psyche set reeling upon this earth…

(But now I have overtaken myself, have let my excitement get the better of me, have become intoxicated by the sight of this confession, now emerging! Yes, confession:

how long have I yearned to express (yes, express and release!) that torrent always raging within the closed confines of my skull; the blessed promise of absolution seems, even now, ever-nearer!)

And so I begin with fever, raging fever, fever from which I have never been free and to which I invariably return! For even at a young age I was troubled, wracked with anxiety, haunted by an insatiable and ravenous intellect: a dismantling and ever-pursuing criticism that disallowed the unaware and contented bliss I saw evident in my schoolmates' faces. I do not mean to proclaim my own cleverness! The faculty to which I am referring has little to do with the quantity and breadth of my knowledge but rather with a certain quality of thought, a 'stance of mind' which saw me bored with some subjects and frantic with others: saw me (in what empty hours remained after the school day was done, and before the cook called for dinner) pursuing my own solitary and oblivious course along wooded paths, so entranced by some progress of ideas that I rarely heard the cook's first (or second, or third!) call…

(But perhaps I have begun again too near in recent history! Should I begin before I was born, begin with my parents' meeting, my conception and progress from tadpole to piglet to human child? Yes, perhaps rightfully I should begin with birth: where else but at a birth does one face oneself? At death: yes, of course at death as well! And how the Absurdist within me laughs each time I consider that it is these mysteries that define one's existence: I imagine others might laugh as well! How ridiculous all else becomes - how much vanity and vexation of the spirit! – when one considers that it remains unknown what life signifies!) Yes, it is better to begin at my birth, to begin with a mystery!

Ah, but such a beginning promises only resignation, only *mauvaise foi*: it is a mystery which can only be solved by postulation, surrender, *ein seliger Sprung in die Ewigkeit*!

Yes, perhaps it is too vast a mystery, and one which pertains only insofar as it pertains to everyone… I will return to it later!)

## 2

Perhaps you already understand that I cannot relate my *ensemble*'s beginning without first explaining that I was a wretched and nervous boy, a boy hounded by relentless inquisitiveness and ever-dismantling thought, inclined toward solitude, unloved by his schoolmates and left alone! For of what use is one given over to his thoughts to those for whom the world is for footraces and games of catch-the-crook, to those who snicker and laugh when the teacher's back is turned? None; he is of no use!

(Of course you do not understand: Costard's transgression, Hermione's yearning, Leontes' searching, Claudio's fall all lay before you! You cannot possibly know what link exists until, like me, these poor set pieces have enacted their ridiculous and improbable drama before you, have slipped from time into the ether of thought; even then I doubt that you will understand! (Yes it is pride you detect in my tone; pride that no other owns a mind such as my own! Even now I know that you will not understand; even now I stumble forward in blind and oft-disappointed hope that these words will find a sympathetic other!)

Even so I do not intend to relate the story of my youth or juvenilia, the poor products of those lonely years; nor is it my intention to convey my progress from curious child to adolescent wounded soul (my first immature yearnings to express, to confess my unhappy state and be absolved!) to aesthetic student, arriving finally at what can only be called man: I have no wish to justify what attempts have come before! I remained one apart, given over to my notions, crowded by the ever-circling and ever-pursuing whirlwind of my thoughts; I lived within my own head, the solitary occupant of a single room from which, looking out, the world appeared foreign and strange, and not entirely belonging to myself (nor I to it).

Is it too much to hope that you, too, have felt this strangeness?)

And naturally you have come to anticipate that my solitude - my eccentric isolation and voluntary seclusion - brought with it the ridicule of my peers: how I remember their barbs! (Yet I do not mean to bemoan the difficulties of my childhood; I do not seek sympathy! Their ridicule was certainly no worse than that suffered by thousands of others at the hands of similar mobs (it was certainly no worse than that which, I have no doubt, others are suffering even as I write this!); no, I do not mean to hoist my childhood above all others and declare it a great trial, a gauntlet from which I emerged as Lazarus, to speak profound truths! I mean only to relate that their ridicule inspired me to divorce myself further from the world, to become moreso the occupant of my thoughts, from wherein I observed the customs and rituals of those with whom I found myself, as though a traveler amongst some savage race…)

## 3

When did I first feel the strangeness to which I have alluded? When did it first occur to me that these rituals were laughable, that I was not their supplicant but their superior? When did I first realize that my life arose from and would return to a mystery, that a thousand cultures had existed (with as much certainty of their self-evidence!) as that which my family called its own, that time spent in misery (my morning's cold shower, the uncomfortable uniform, the tedious schoolwork, my classmates' relentless cruelties) would not be returned to me? (When did the Absurd Man first open his eyes?) It is so hard to know! I have no doubt, at least, that it occurred to me long before I read those works which echoed these same conclusions (long before I knew that my Absurd Man had a name!), for I clearly recall that those words upon the page were to me not a revelation but a relief (for in the words of those long-dead writers I found something like a compatriot spirit)...

Regardless, it was only in my teenage years that this revelation became coupled with militance, only then that the laughter accompanying my private criticism (the laughter which echoed, in repulsion, within my mind at each new superstition discovered and each strange custom exposed) found voice...

Yes, found voice: but not as laughter! For as the laughter passed from my thoughts to my lips it became instead a frantic scribbling: slippery thoughts spawned concrete words; my notebook became my constant companion; it was never far from my side! (Did this invite further ridicule? Yes, naturally! And yet in time I came to welcome it: their ridicule echoed my own inner assertion that I was not one like them, that their world held no claim upon me! If I was an outcast then so be it: it was best to be an outcast, uninitiated into their life's poor offerings! It is here you find the origin of my pride!)

## 4

I have said that there exists within me something I have called Artist: and now you see the interwoven tangle of my soul! For the Artist owns no words but feelings, just as the Absurd Man owns only calculated thought… What is one without the other? And how can I be certain that the Absurd Man did not birth the Artist so that he might express himself… Ah, madness: such brazen madness!

I yet suspect that there is nothing within me, no impulse, which might not have one day been otherwise sublimated into the day-to-day troubles of a banker or a shopkeeper: how joyous – how sane – that track appears to me now! What a happy life I might have lived, but for the Absurd Man and the Artist whispering together in my dark interior… (But of course it is ridiculous to consider such alternatives: have I not claimed, regardless, a Devil and Savior within me as well? Would a banker's worries have silenced their torments? No: certainly they would not!)

Yet I hear you protesting: such ethereal troubles; give us something real! Indeed, you are right to protest: do not think that I have not chastised myself for the same, and worse! I am guilty – yes, relentlessly, repeatedly guilty! – of the most indulgent flights: I unapologetically stand as both protagonist and antagonist! You are right to decry such indulgence!

Ah yes, the real! A ring of faces: older and drooping, mouths wetted by dark liquors, prehensile bones grasping cut crystal and fingering brass buttons; the panel - the eternal jury – of my father's friends! Do you balk at this presentation, call them less substantive for having long since become hobgoblins in my mind? But listen; I am trying to tell you something!

I have said that the ceaseless mill of my thoughts might have yet been quieted by some pedestrian course, subdued by degrees until its racing current traversed only the petty concerns of office, home, wife, children… And yet I shrank from this path, declared it lower: to what do I owe the luxury of this disdain? I hear your laughter and yet shout over it with all my breath: it is to this panel that I owe my arrogance, to them I owe this pride! For I own the misfortune of having been praised solely, through these lonely middle years, for those odd ends of prose brought by this-or-that tutor, this-or-that teacher, to my parents' attention: and from my parents, to my father's friends: can you know what it is to have the cold and cruel and indifferent world suddenly turn its benevolent gaze upon you? No: you cannot imagine that all-encompassing bliss! Is it odd that these moments of parental embrace (embrace that was more than embrace, for it embraced also my unique interior!) became the secret aim of my pitiful endeavors, the highest goal of my vague and immature ramblings…

(And so you say now that I write always as a child, hoping always to earn some ethereal maternal regard… Perhaps you are correct!)

Yes: if not for damning early praise I might have ceased in my efforts; what artist has not considered that he might have been happier, after all, had those early supporters instead turned their attentions elsewhere, convinced him by their indifference to leave off his aspirations for other, less lonely paths? With what all-enraptured joy I recited to those my father gathered; with what stoic pride I received their applause! (You cannot imagine what it was to hear from a panel of superiors that that which had earned my exile was in fact that which would hoist me above all others: to hear it murmured that such talent was uncharacteristic in one so young, that I was certain to produce great art!)

How many other follies owe their origin to the too-serious regard for the brandied and over-excited mutterings of one's betters? And how often I have wished since that I had turned them a deaf ear! (Yes: for to me art is a flame to which one holds oneself, an Icarian flight melting away falsehoods as waxen feathers; how often did I rise from my childhood desk at dawn, sleepless and trembling, the newly-written page like some pagan idol before me? How many forgone meals were left outside my door?) Yes, certainly it would have been better to receive no praise at all, to surrender to the world's indifference!

Yet such was not the case, my ramblings won me praise; this-or-that friend of my father's knew the editor of the newspaper, this other friend knew someone at a national magazine; my stories began to appear in print (how clearly I remember the intoxication of holding the first in my hands!) and it was not long before the town, the city (indeed, it soon seemed, the whole world!) echoed with the whispered exclamation that such talent was uncharacteristic in one so young, that certainly I would produce great work...)

## 5

Yet through it all the Absurd Man stood as a stranger upon a foreign shore, sickled o'er by mystery and made supplicant to a vast and impenetrable absurdity. No praise or parental soothing, no kind or sympathetic word, no compatriot spirit could brighten his joyless world with compassionate pathos! (Yes: the intoxication I felt at their praise was soon dismantled by his assertion of its meaninglessness, and further disparaged by the ever-lurking Devil! For what, he sneered, did these small-town simpletons know of Art? Their praise counted for nothing against the canon! Perhaps (I was tormented by the thought!) their accolades indicated the lowness of my efforts, that they would appeal to ones such as these!)

I have called this lonely and self-exiling state my pride and yet must confess that the brief moments of intoxication (moments in which their praise was undiminished by the Devil's laughter, by the Absurd Man's dismissal) were to me the sweetest moments of life; and so I must confess (yes confess, but have already revealed!) that within my proud exile I felt (and could not silence!) a yearning which revealed me to myself (how I wished that I was free from it, had overcome it!): that I wanted this comfort, that I sought relief! Yes: even as I laughed at their rituals I could not fully mute the quadrant of my heart which longed to be embraced among them, to live a life such as theirs, to believe in their ordered existence, in their (beautifully!) clear conception of heaven and earth; their embrace (to be gathered in among them, a sheep returned to the fold!) seemed to me more precious, more holy than all the Sunday sermons I'd heard and crosses I'd seen…

This yearning (yearning that was both a yearning to be embraced by them and also to embrace that which they embraced) startled and horrified me: I remained a human being like them, inherently weak in mind and vulnerable in body, woefully prone to pleasant fairy tales of blessed eternity… No, I could not deny that my heart beat just as theirs! What a horror it was to me then: to see something of myself in the leering faces of my tormentors!

(And with this yearning came a sublimated second: that I might be embraced by one among them, and find in her arms something of that absolution promised by heaven and yet denied to me (for I could not believe in their God: even in moments of exhaustion and weakness I could not will myself to that ignorance, could not call down that blindness!); to what do I attribute this fantasy? My mother, finding me heartsick and lonely (my brothers and sisters, otherwise engaged, left me often to my own devices), promised that there existed for everyone a perfect other in whom the heart found absolution and peace: ridiculous! and yet I perceive the seed of that promise in the color and tenor of the desires that followed…

For I did not feel my classmates' egalitarian cravings! The sight of those most-coveted girls often produced in me only disinterest (or sometimes a mild nausea); all their beauty of form seemed to me irreparably tainted by a vast and seething undercurrent of worldliness. How I longed for one who saw, as I saw, the world's laughable absurdity, its profound horror! (Covered in filth, wretched, she would have appeared to me yet more lovely than the Madonna herself…)

(And I now recall my most cherished fantasy from that time: that I might leave my notebook somewhere and become panicked that it would be found by one of my peers, that his cruel and ignorant eyes might peruse my most intimate thoughts, my most hidden heart! I would rush back to the last place I remembered having it; a girl (through the years this savior took on the face of several different girls) would be holding it in her hands; she had not known there was another who felt as she did! She had not understood, and yet how she loved me now…)

Laughable! And yet it was these fantasies alone that sustained me through a joyless and seemingly interminable existence…)

## 6

How I longed to leave that town, to leave my childhood life behind! The vast unexplored world called to me from beyond the threshold of my never-nearer eighteenth year (yes, called to me, held the promise of relief and absolution in some as-yet unexplored temple, some far-off mountaintop…); I longed for clarity, for relief, for a reflection (like the face of God!) to present itself! (I have named Artist and Devil, Savior and Absurd Man, and yet to which does this searching belong? None: I must call this seeker by another name, must call the seeker Child: yes, I sought in the world something of that all-encompassing embrace I first perceived standing before that eternal jury, that embrace the child feels when suckling its mother's breast, something of that embrace my lonely path denied!)

How clearly I recall the joy I felt when that morning finally arrived, knowing that I was to leave! (And how much more profound the sorrow I feel now in recalling it, knowing that the journey it began has ended here!)

I have already explained that I saw little reflection of myself in my classmates' faces, found there no compatriot spirit; is it strange to suggest that it was something of this compatriot spirit that I sought in the face of the mountains or the sky? (Is it strange to state that it was something of that same isolation I felt while I watched Pacific breakers strike the Peruvian shore, observed flocks of birds moving north, while I weathered the monsoon? Is it strange that these sights should inspire loneliness? What is God, after all, but man's projection of his own reflection upon the universe, the mask of a familiar face designed to defang the vast and horrific mystery? I must admit that I sought something of this same recognition…)

Yes! Each new monument and shore, each new jungle and sunset brought with it euphoric anticipation within which I blinded myself to all previous disappointments (so many disparate and strange experiences, and yet each brought with it a familiar disappointment!). I pinned my hopes on each new thing's promise and yet each new place taunted me with its subsequent denial (how Hamlet-like my ramblings from that time! For I find in those notebooks a hundred stages declared sterile promontories, a thousand Elsinores, each a prison…); it serves no purpose to recall them all! Only my frustration remains. After two years of travel my disappointment overwhelmed my hope; I could rouse neither interest nor inspiration sufficient to make this-or-that journey, witness this-or-that equinox, stand beneath this-or-that sky…

How barren - how worthless - my life appeared! And how beautiful the ordered world! How devoutly I wished to surrender beneath the church's illuminated ceiling, cast myself upon the courthouse steps, subjugate myself to the tedium and rigor of a work-a-day life! Would that I could have surrendered to these delusions, these brazen assertions of compatriot spirit pasted on boundless and meaningless infinity...

(I am certain it comes as no surprise to you, then, that at times I wished only to end my anxiety: I contemplated various devices, stood upon the precipice and considered the storming sea below, drank to excess with the vague notion of producing a stupor from which I would not emerge...)

## 7

How black those days appear to me now! Yet that darkness is of such a peculiar quality that I can see it only from without: encamped in this-or-that jungle, nestled amongst the rocks of this-or-that desert I looked only to the next meal, the next path; I lived with my eyes cast to the earth for fear that, looking skyward, I would find revealed there the articulated promise of my barren future! Indeed, it was only after I had abandoned my travels that I understood my own despair (how I pitied myself my doomed searching! How little I had understood my own heart! Nothing can now be done: youth is the time for such doomed dogmas, and one is certain to recall one's hopes with bitterness and shame for the ignorant paths one set oneself upon!)

But enough! All of this is only to preface what followed. On furlough from my searching (I had been violently ill, and returned to the city only with careful assistance, where I was left in a hostel to convalesce) I stumbled one Algerian evening down a street all but deserted: a solitary man stood (as though entranced) some distance from me; graceless in my as-yet unresolved illness (and feeling also, therefore, more potently the supper wine) I approached him; his eyes were cast upward to where I, following their gaze, discerned also a woman standing at her window, in the throes of impassioned singing… And yet, how strange! For save for the sounds of the street behind and before (what little there was of it: the shops were closing, few cars rode the pavement) there was no other sound: the woman's voice (though offered *con brio!*) was wholly muted by both glass and distance. (The man did not acknowledge me, the woman give no indication of any awareness of our presence; I stumbled on, casting only one final, fascinated glance in parting…)

How that image haunted me, sickened me, lured me! The fever and wine-haze were insufficient to erase it from my mind (indeed seemed only to implant it more firmly, just as I have heard those in a fever sometimes become transfixed by images and phrases, repeating them endlessly!): the man's glazed and glassy eyes, the woman's violent and emotive gestures, and the silence: the absurd and ever-present silence! So profoundly was I impressed by this pair that my convalescent hours seem now, in memory, characterized by this single experience: I can recall neither room nor bed, but would recognize both man and woman in a crowd tomorrow as though my own brother and sister, my own mother and father…

## 8

I will attempt to describe what so confronted and confounded me! I have already made some explanation of the Absurd Man, related that even as a child I beheld the world's inherent insubstantiality: that I sensed the essential ridiculousness of my peers' rituals and superstitions, found that I lacked the capacity for religion: the world, therefore, in all its politics and fashions, its modes and postures, confronted and baffled me, seemed to me a vast and teeming sty wherein each rutting sow and hog held the absurd belief that their rutting and burrowing occurred beneath heaven's gaze and with His subtle affirmation (thus I felt myself at odds with the world, attuned to a profound and ever-present truth whose apprehension was reserved for a select few)… And yet I hear you protest, for was it not something very like a religious impulse which compelled me deeper into deserts and jungles, into mountains and across oceans? Have I not already admitted that I sought something not unlike the face of God? Yes, you are correct! Yes: for nearly two years my heart gave itself over wholly to the Child, kept faith in seeking: for two years I entertained my irrepressible human yearning to believe! And yet after two years my heart became exhausted: I could no longer sustain the faith that I might find that for which I searched, that ever-retreating *desideratum*…

Exhausted and delirious the man's glassy and transfixed eyes, the woman's silence struck me strangely: how do I describe it? The Absurd Man opened his eyes within my own: the meaningful matrix upon which the street, the buildings, the town, country, continent, race rested was, for a moment (yes, only a moment, but somehow timeless as well!) blotted out, leaving only an inarticulate jumble of physical remnants, of artifacts from an unknown and unknowable civilization (though the civilization was my own!); I felt suddenly that horrible freedom (that no ideologies (I had laughed at ideologies but nevertheless feared them, subjugated myself to them!) could claim me), saw in place of the world a barren promenade…

## 9

The Absurd Man: doubtless you have already discerned the origin of this name! Do not think that I borrow from Camus frivolously: rather, I do so with guileless intention! For it is in Camus as well that one finds an inappropriate silence, a revelation of the absurd: a man is speaking on a telephone behind a glass partition; the glass mutes the man's voice; his gestures, the movements of his face, tongue, lips, divested of the meaning his words would give them, appear mechanical, inhuman; he is a grotesque pantomime; the *stage set collapses!*

(And life has since cast such doubt upon my overwrought mind: do I find here the beginning of my delusion and madness? Did I really stumble, half-crazed, down an Algerian street? Did I, in fact, come upon this strange scene? Or was it rather a fever dream, within which memories of the town's alleys and occupants mixed with fragments of long-since-read philosophy to produce a cathartic fantasy… I do not know; I do not know!)

Such is, perhaps, of little consequence: when I emerged from my fever I had lost all desire for travel, had no more faith in searching; likewise I could find reason to neither stay nor leave, to journey elsewhere or wait out my remaining years: was this despair? Certainly: I felt crushingly the weight of my failed years; I lay upon my cot, feeling unworthy of breath…

But one cannot live thusly: the animal body asserts itself when the higher mind is brought to distraction! I became motivated by hunger, by thirst, by an irrepressible loneliness; I ventured forth into the world with shame that I was of such base nature! (Indeed, that the singular authority of my despair might be so easily usurped by these primal yearnings disgusted me, revealed me to myself as peasant, philistine, man…)

## 10

And now you see me loathe myself my humanity, and call me a hater of man! But such is hardly the case: it is not man that I hate but men, the striving throng, the violent horde, the cacophonous mass reciting their rote prayers to reticent heaven and finding in it's perambulations the justification for their horrid ways… Yes it is men that I despise, men that I fear and loathe: the mob gathered into simple frenzy wherein my heart's panicked objections can find no voice or ear, the crowd congregated as walls made deaf by dogma and cruel by fear… Yes, certainly I hate men! But man: no, I do not hate man! For in man is the chance of salvation: could I find but one other to whom I might explain, one other to know my thoughts, one in whom my anguished heart might find its mirror… Ah, such would be the ecstasy of absolution, the communal wafer, Eden's bliss…

Ah yes: my boyhood fantasy! That the Beatrice of the moment would find my misplaced notebook and absolve its contents with the anointing oil of her embrace… I hear your criticism again ringing in my ears, that I write always as a child! (If you are correct your insight, even as damning censure, falls upon me as sweet relief: that I might untangle the confused web of my thoughts, and find therein a single moment of clarity, of peace... But I have again overtaken myself!)

# 11

I wandered the streets in half-daze, half-dream: how do I describe the sensation that accompanied my meandering course? You have, no doubt, perceived a thing with the edges of your vision, only to turn and find it absent? How much more maddening, when that half-glimpsed thing is not a thing at all! For I wandered the streets in search of that same experience again, searched hoping that some magical coupling of light and lamppost, of building and beech tree might again awaken me to certainty of the world's weightlessness. (Turning this-or-that corner, confronted by this-or-that frontispiece, I felt the Absurd Man stir within me; yet when I turned that elusive whisper had vanished, leaving him to settle down into slumber and me to grasp at remembered sensations as at a rapidly-retreating dream…)

How frustrating those days! For I felt myself always on the verge of epiphany, felt as though insight lay just beyond the next streetlamp, the far cobbled corner, the ocean's shore…

(And yes: now you laugh and call me dramatic, a fool acting the tragedian! For what differentiates my searching in those days from the searching that preceded it, the searching that drove me to traverse the globe? Nothing, certainly: how laughable, then, my despair! For certainly I was not so desperate as I claimed or imagined myself to be! Yes: you laugh and are right to laugh! Perhaps I am not the tragic figure, the *ubermensch* wandering alone but rather the fool, so absorbed in his own ridiculous thoughts that he does not notice, while imagining himself above, that he is eternally beneath!

But I am not the fool; I must believe that I am not the fool! No, I am not a fool, or the sins I have committed find no justification in their end, in these pages: I must not be a fool lest I admit finally to madness, surrender to the despair that these pages will find no regarding eye nor sympathetic ear! (For of what value can the works of my hands be, if I am a fool?) No, they must be something more!)

It was within this fever - this maddening frenzy - that my poor cast began in earnest! For after several days (I had stumbled from cafe to bar to bed; my notebook was with me always) I penned the following line:

> She considered her life: each aspect rested on another, was undercut by its arbitrary predecessor in a deconstructive chain leading back to the blank canvas, to defenseless impulse and unjustifiable whim. She felt seduced by despair, felt a void opening before her; what was this void? The apparition of suicide, the specter of her own death? No, it was the nothingness stretching forever beneath the seemingly concrete aspects of her existence, the eternal blank canvas upon which she had enacted her life (and to which she would eventually return)...

Yes: I wrote the line (how the sight of it intoxicates me still!) and then tore frantically through my pages, searching for its twin... Eventually I found it; the sight of it horrified and enlivened me: I was certain in that moment that I was mad - finally mad! – and yet equally certain that this madness was in fact the waxen wings that would carry me from my interminable worldly prison... (But here now is that passage!)

> The familiar structure of his week suddenly confronted and overwhelmed him. How arbitrary it all seemed! Each aspect rested upon and buttressed the others, yet taken together they existed within no broader meaningful frame necessitating their form. Why this thing, and why not this other? A thousand disassociated

> happenings had produced a life at once self-contained and insubstantial: his life was like a spider's web forced from its housing by the wind and now drifting on the empty air, intact!

And here again!

> The telephone woke him: his wife had been so worried! And why hadn't he called when he arrived? Speaking softly (his mistress was still asleep beside him) he explained that his luggage had been lost, and he had simply forgotten in the confusion. Hanging up he felt a strange sensation; he could see neither floor nor opposite wall (he had not turned on the bedside light), and he imagined that the darkness before him was not the shadows of his hotel room but was rather Oblivion swelling like the sea to swallow him, a pit which had miraculously opened at his feet and into which he was now falling… He was hypnotized by that seemingly vast emptiness beneath him…

I have already made clear illustration of my own fragmented mind, the many selves that occupy my frame: it should not surprise you then that in these characters these fragments fragmenting further, grew faces and names: grew indeed to become autonomous others describing my sublimated past and my unrealized future, my dreams and nightmares! (And the image of the man's hollow and transfixed eyes, his half-hanging mouth, the woman's broad sweeping and utterly ridiculous gestures had inspired within me an acute and irrepressible – an overwhelming and cacophonous! - response, as though all these inhabitants arose at once (whether in triumphant shouting or vehement condemnation!) at the very slightest glimpse of that memory…)

## 12

I rented a small room, I shunned outside contact; I positioned myself at my writing table and held myself to the flame. For how long? For how many hours, days, weeks? I have no memory, nor way of knowing: over-stimulated by travel and constantly-shifting horizons, made weak by prolonged illness the sight of bare, changeless walls comforted me, lulled me easily into a dreamy state within which I had no awareness of day or night… How strange it was, to look to the sun and see the moon there instead! How often I awoke in confusion on the narrow cot, unsure whether the hour on the clock's face referred to morning or evening, day or night…

I ate and slept little, stopped shaving (what little beard I had grew tangled and wild), I became paler still; eventually I was so transformed that, upon entering a shop, the sight of my own reflection in the window glass seemed to me (for one horrid and yet joyful moment) not my own but that of a stranger. (Yes, and with what madman gusto I laughed then! The other patrons hurried past me, did not stop to inquire as to the cause of my merriment…)

But perhaps I became a madman! If madness is that blessed inability to reconcile oneself to the world then certainly I was mad then, have always been mad, remain mad! (And yet I declare that I am not mad, that I possess too clear an intellect to give over, finally, to madness (just as I could not, despite my often earnest yearnings, give over to God, to the blessed order of the man-made world, so too I could not and cannot give over my heart to chaos, to absurdity! No, I am not mad, though my circumstances rebuff my claims of reason!)

For how long did I maintain this vigil? When I entered the room the boughs that overhung the river were bare; when I emerged the orange tree in the park had long since dropped its fruit; my final lines were serenaded to their completion by the cacophony of birds picking over what rotten and fermented harvest remained; I clutched the manuscript to my breast and went trembling into the world…

# CANTO TWO § COSTARD

# 1

They insist that I do not excite myself, that I neither exhaust nor exert myself: they do not know what they ask! For I can no more oblige them than I can sprout wings and fly from their pleasant prison: to draw breath is to do so in inspiration, is to bellow the flame in my Artist's heart!

(I hear them calling: they entreat me to extinguish my light! How can I concur? My pages beckon to me like a drunken bride…)

(Yes: I can hardly sleep for reading, for reading and knowing more clearly! For myself now emerges; I see myself more clearly! The disorder – the chaos! – in my soul grows boundaries and borders with each page my mind consumes; my fevered madness – my disquiet brain! – might find its end in such knowledge…)

And yet now I laugh at these words: I laugh at myself for having penned them! As though I have judged myself possessed by demons, compelled by devils, in need of an exorcism! Nothing so occult emerges! (How I would welcome the occult, some intimation of higher powers, whether for good or ill! Would that I could believe myself set upon by demons, tormented by hell, the protagonist of some otherworldly conflict! My horror would be superceded - would be eternally assuaged! - by the infinite bliss of unquestioning knowing…)

# 2

But perhaps now you understand! Perhaps now you understand that I am myself inextricable from these poor sublimations: that their pedestrian woes mean little without my exegesis! Their troubles, their successes and failures, mean little but for *that which I have attempted to capture through them*; they are the arrows I shot toward distant heaven, which I launched to fell God Himself! (But no, you are correct: I do not refer to the God of churches and steeples, of stained glass and cruciform wood! My arrows I shot into the ether, into the firmament, into black space and unknowable mystery! From what had my life arisen? Into what would it return? How many cultures had existed (with as much certainty of their self-evidence!) as my own? And how many immortal Gods now found their temples destroyed by time, the worshipers returned to dust? O Gods, I compel you like Ahab to answer me! Halt my blasphemies if you are able!)

(Even now I surprise myself: even now I am revealed! For how strange that I should, in heated rambling, equate my words to arrows, my arrows to blasphemies… And yet perhaps I know why! For as a child I received, as a birthday gift, a child's bow and arrow: wandering alone upon some wooded path I heard the birds singing and, fancying myself the stealthy hunter, let fly; what horror that chance should so conspire! For one detached itself from the flock, and fell… I followed the sound of its calling (for what reason? My body ached to flee, to put those terrible cries far behind!); it lay upon the earth (even now I am confronted by its horrible size, the blackness of its feathers, the viciousness of its wheeling, searching eyes!); as I watched it stood, attempted to rise into the air; it was no use, my arrow had broken its wing; its terrible croaking cry filled my ears! Finally I compelled my feet to turn; I ran with the irrational certainty that its compatriots had returned, compelled by its cries to pursue me, to enact – to extract! - bloody recompense…

And yet that is not all! For I returned beneath the eaves of my father's house in an absurd calm, made no display of agitation (nor, I suspect would my agitation have produced any effect: both mother and father were forever occupied elsewhere!); I walked through those hallways as a condemned man, certain that my crime would find me out: yes, the gardener was certain to find the felled bird, the cook was certain to hear its cries! I walked in a daze, waiting for the ax to fall…

And yet no discovery came, no punishment occurred! For two days I waited for some mention to be made, some otherworldly omen to declare my guilt; I wandered as in a fevered daze, as though unhinged from the world. How the secret tore at my interior! My days I spent wretched upon the divan, my nights I passed in dreams that the felled bird I carried somehow inside myself, behind my ribs: that it beat its broken wing and tore at my fragile heart and lungs, my soft flesh with beak and talons…

I yearned for discovery, for punishment to absolve me! And yet soon my mind turned upon itself, I began to mock my own guilty heart; to what insane quadrant do I assign this impetus? Was it the Devil, driving me toward superior loneliness? Or was it, rather, the Absurd Man's infantile stirrings? I can only say that I soon found myself inspired with what can only be called disdain: yes, my parents' company soon excited my wonder at their ignorance! (What terrible power for a child to feel! And yet: how could I help but loathe them that they were not there to punish me, to smash my arrows, to sever my bowstrings? And how could I not hate my guilty heart which, as I took my first terrible, tentative steps (beyond judgment, beyond right and wrong!) threatened to confess: to subjugate itself once more beneath the heavy word of law? You see that I must be torn!)

And now you repeat your accusation: that I write always as a child seeking some ethereal maternal regard! Yes, I say to you; yes I fire my words like arrows upward seeking that near boundary of heaven! O Gods, rain down fire, else declare openly your impotence!

# 3

You have concluded, no doubt, that I am irredeemable, that my pages comprise only so much self-glory, that my regard for my own thoughts blinds me to their undeniably banal and prosaic quality! And yet you are mistaken, for I have in fact written these paragraphs for your benefit: they comprise only a prelude to what I have designed to follow after! For without this parable Costard's transgression loses its soul; to deny you this history is to deny you illumination! (Yes it is pride you detect in my tone: I marvel now at my own cleverness! Perhaps you suggest that there is a Rooster inside me as well, who struts his meager barnyard and imagines himself king of all the world! And yet you are again mistaken, if you assert that this pride comprises yet another facet to my already divided interior: no, this pride is my Artist's!)

But enough; I have said enough! Costard requires no further introduction than what has already been stated, requires no more overture than that which has already been provided in the telling of my dual horrors (a man stands beneath a window, transfixed; an arrow shot upward reveals the Gods' indifference); the Artist within me seized upon these, extracted from them the essential and eternal; it was only later that the details that would define him arose, later that he was given a name…

(I leave off my explication and preface! Here are those pages!)

> …Settling into his middle years, well-established in life, he stood beneath the bookstore's second-story window behind which a girl, unaware of her audience, sang: the thickness of the glass and the distance muted her; the street and surrounding sidewalk were empty; he

wondered what she was singing, felt an overwhelming desire to know...

His students' questions, office hours, Monday morning department meeting, Sunday laundry, the weekly rotation of dinners, the familiar quiet in the hour before bed, the brief litany of conversations, the alternate mornings driving his son to school: the familiar structure of his week suddenly confronted and overwhelmed him. How arbitrary it all seemed! Each aspect rested upon and buttressed the others, yet taken together they existed within no broader meaningful frame necessitating their form. Why this thing, and why not this other? A thousand disassociated happenings had produced a life at once self-contained and insubstantial: his life was like a spider's web forced from its housing by the wind and now drifting on the empty air, intact!

What would it be like to live alone on the Riviera, to explore Africa, to attempt any number of preemptively dismissed endeavors? Such lives, after all, were lived by men not unlike himself! He stood before no eternal and disallowing jury, anticipated no postmortem judgment; there was no jury before whom to stand, no judge in whose name to act! Yes: life was a prolonged madness encased within indiminishable ignorance: how many cultures had existed and faded into extinction with as much certainty of their own self-evidence as that which he called his own? (And his own: how banal, how base it seemed! And yet his youthful refusal of its ignoble characteristics had all but faded in the name of comfort; yes! The ascetic impulse that had applauded the scholastic life and hoisted it above all others was now a mildly embarrassing memory, an emblem of naiveté emblazoned across his youthful years, long since forgone! And yet, having dismissed the purported rewards of such a life (he knew better now than to think that enlightenment came through study!) his life became only a shell of familiar behaviors, enacted with no hope of progress, made palatable only through distraction and insidious ease!

Yes: his life was a comfortably appointed room whose windows looked out onto brick and mortar walls and whose doors opened onto barren deserts and wasted fields: it held nothing for him!)

He awoke as from a dream: how long had he been standing, watching her? He hardly knew: he had been entranced! He felt a sudden panic: what if she had seen him? And what if she should see him now, and stop? The thought of this artless intrusion and its predictable and awkward result brought him fully back to himself. He turned and walked quickly away.

Nearing his car, he realized suddenly why the girl had so fascinated him: she was the exact image of a former student of his, a girl with whom he had become particularly close! So profound was the resemblance that he was momentarily certain that it was the same girl. Yet he recognized almost immediately (he had turned back towards the book store, but now turned again and returned to his car) that it could not be the same person: that girl had been his student nearly ten years ago, while the girl singing at the window was certainly no older than twenty!

This fact startled and confronted him. Was it possible that ten years had passed? There was no mistaking it: he had come to the university before her senior term, and was now concluding his eleventh year. Impossible! Where had the time gone? He remembered the girl so clearly! And yet it occurred to him that, barring any accident, she was older now than he was then, when she had sat in his classroom as a student.

(And he himself was older! Ten years: ten stagnated years! What had he accomplished in that time? What had occurred? Nothing: he had done nothing! He had been piling life upon life, repeating endlessly a progression that had been determined more than a decade before…)

## 4

And who was the girl of ten years earlier? And what did their relationship entail? Nothing: what occurred between them was chaste as a sonnet! For he felt, at the time, that the body's presence was an encumbrance to the union of minds, that its impulses were base, animal… How he laughed now at his own lofty and academic abstinence: a philosophical eunuch, convinced that something greater could be achieved with words!

Yet his laughter here is my own, and directed at none but myself: I was the chaste thinker, the mind lamenting its primal casing, sickened by my body's insistence, its yearning, its hunger and thirst; how I longed to overcome and negate the body! (From what does this repulsion arise? I can recall with vivid horror early childhood excursions to the shore: the conglomeration of commingled flesh in various stages of youth and decline, multifarious and yet uniform, an inescapable classification as though I, a butterfly, found myself bearing the regrettable markings of a dung beetle! Yes: and my own mother and father, my siblings - myself! – all one brotherhood of reprehensible humanity (for what was humanity if not that which knelt before insane altars, which turned its power against those it might, which rutted at bawds and declared itself superior?); was it any wonder that I refused my bathing clothes, that I wandered aloof, my flesh obscured by heavy garments, taking what little comfort I might in this minor distinction…)

I have already related that I did not share my schoolmates' indiscriminate visceral yearnings, that it was always the fantasy of another in whose mind I might discover thoughts the reflection of my own that excited me, encouraged me, sustained me; and yet how should I perform when confronted by one such as this? How I laugh to recall my own unpracticed *conduite sociale*! For in my final year of schooling I was unexpectedly roused from my solitude by lips parting in question; what did I think of this-or-that work? She had observed me reading and, assuming that it must be of some special interest (I had a reputation, by then, for being the intellectual superior of my schoolmates, and inclined toward headier tomes), read it herself: yet she hardly knew what to make of it; what did I think of this-or-that? And what did I make of this-or-that other?

How clearly I recall the intoxication of that first meeting! Having for so long resigned myself to the shell of interaction (I responded correctly but succinctly to my instructors; my parents, assuming it was my wish, kept sacred my solitude, and inquired little after my affairs) I marveled at the (I must call it) verbose outpouring that followed! For it was long after the period bell had rung that I concluded my diatribe, fueled onward at every pause by her eager questions, her excited assertions…

Ah, but naturally you assume what can only be obvious: this memory is too colored by emotion, too fantastic to have occurred in the manner that I claim! I am certain that you are correct, and yet can find no other memory to refute its authority: it has been reshaped by fond reuse, just as the ocean remakes the stones it caresses! It will perhaps suffice, then, to relate only the import, and as such to reduce it little with my own daydreaming lens: we became fast compatriots; my scribbling ceased, my thoughts found voice; soon I felt (in her silent response, in her gesture; in a thousand ways that I, grown attuned, could not ignore) a yearning; spring arrived, my departure beckoned, and still I pretended ignorance, returning to the subject at hand when in her silence I sensed a nervous and excited possibility…

Why, you ask? Do not think that I have not asked the same! (Yes, asked: and tormented myself in asking! For this boundary, now reached, soon encapsulated and lessened all that had preceded it: as my departure neared she pursued me less; summer had arrived, and she found less time for reading those volumes I suggested, less time for the morose contemplation I insisted lay at the heart of true insight (and thus at the heart of true union)… What disdain I came to feel when, finding myself again alone, I grouped her with the others, called her shallow, base, vacuous, and comforted myself with the grand metaphor that she was unworthy of my Icarian flight, that her feathers had melted and she had fallen to the sea… How I laugh to think of it now (a cruel laughter, that mocks my own tears)! And how quickly I came to harbor nostalgia for that unsanctified union, and with it hatred for that ridiculous and immature stance that finds one unable to reconcile one's angel with one's lover!)

(But enough, I hear you cry: enough! What of Costard? What of the girl singing behind the glass? Are you so poor a poet as to leave your characters thus sketched, a single image in a series, the rest dissolved? Indeed you are correct: I lament such artless intrusion! I leave off recollection and return to Costard!)

His thoughts wandered and returned to the girl:
he felt again that his life had been arbitrarily composed,
that it remained insubstantial; this sense (that his life
had followed one of many paths, that it was one of

innumerable possibilities) brought with it a needling curiosity: what would it be like to live this-or-that life, or this-or-that other? Clinging ever-closer to the classroom, he had preemptively dismissed them (he might do such-and-such at some time in the future, but now he had this paper to write, this thesis to finish, these papers to grade!), composing instead a life which now required his continuing fealty and disallowed all others. But these others, now vaguely considered, seemed wonders whose honeyed promises (certainly this-or-that life would be bliss! And this-or-that other!) devalued own his life...

His life confronted him always on all sides! His wife's sister wanted her daughter to stay with them for the summer! His son had been sneaking out at night! The head of the department wanted a meeting with him! And his students' papers needed grading; this one wanted to meet with him after class! And this one needed more time!

Indeed, his life held nothing for him! Sunday laundry, the weekly rotation of dinners, the customary quiet in the hour before bed, the brief litany of conversations: the familiar structure of his familiar life bored and horrified him. The order which had seemed, for years, infinitely fragile (how carefully he had crafted himself into a Professor in no way objectionable, and certain to become tenured; how delicately he had composed himself as father, orbiting the world of mother and son!) now burdened him with its immutable walls, promised only repetitive exercise and joyless effort. How empty his books and insights! How laughable his academic striving, his progressless movement in the ether, pursuing only his own thoughts! (And how often was he forced to disguise his contempt for this-or-that of his wife's behaviors? How often had he silenced his protesting heart? Too often: too often by far!)

Yes! He longed for a change, a transformation potent enough to unmake his wasted years...

(His wife rolled against him in her sleep, her graceless bulk repulsed him; half-waking, she placed her head on his shoulder. He did not move but escaped into dreams in which the singing girl was both departure and destination for a complex and evolving fantasy: one in which his life and its familiar demands were left behind, in which he pursued numerous implausible endeavors, from which his wife and her son were wholly absent.)

## 5

But now the Devil within me laughs, calls this fiction artless, uninspired! (How earnest and laughable my efforts seem, when reconsidered, dissected; how I loathe myself, recalling with what self-satisfied and proud posturing I first penned them!) Doubtless you have perceived the guileless impetus of my rambling: the Sirens, too, lured men to their destruction, inspired Ulysses to cast himself upon the rocky shores! (Yes, perhaps the Artist in me holds such poor ability that his cleverness amounts only to obvious reference and reclaimed and fragmentary philosophies (I did not, after all, give the Absurd Man his name!)...)

Yes, it is in invocation of the Sirens that I composed Costard: I can offer no other cause for his subsequent fascination! For what is a girl, noiselessly singing behind glass? A novelty, and nothing more, and easily dismissed! Doubtless you assert that his interest signifies nothing, that such strange episodes are liable to linger in memory, that one need not dismantle one's life over such trivialities! I can offer no refutation! Naturally you are correct! I must call my *deus ex machina* by its name, and myself a poor Artist for so poor a device!

But perhaps you will forgive me for enacting (like the Olympian Gods!) my own unapologetic machinations and orchestrations: Costard, defined by cowardliness and retreat, certainly could not be trusted solely to enact his own transgression! (How long he might have continued this inactive and covetous vigil, were it not for my intervention? How long had he already silenced his protesting heart? What might I do but cast him, as Poseidon, adrift upon the sea…)

(But I will offer this as well! Recall the story of the blackbird, and imagine in Costard this same long-latent impulse, now awakening! For Costard is none other than myself, and capable of all that I am…)

He returned to the bookshop and watched her. He prayed that she would be called to one of the registers: there, under pretense of buying something, he could easily engage her! But when she stood at the register he was likewise confronted: certainly there were too many others in line, and their interaction would be limited to necessities! On other nights, in the sparsely populated store, he was certain that his lingering presence could not fail to attract notice; feeling obvious and ridiculous for having come, cursing himself that his defining cowardice still so obviously held sway, he returned home…

How he longed to speak with her! The absurdity of this wish in no way reduced his desire. He could not dismiss the lingering hope that he would find within her some echo of that which he had once shared with his former student. Yet this hope further hampered his efforts: simultaneously aware that she was not the same girl who had sat in his classroom he hesitated to confront sustaining fantasy with unpleasant truth, preferring instead a distant, growing, and utterly unfounded adoration.

If not for chance, he might have continued! But his students organized a walkout in protest of the war, and there was no class to teach; he went for lunch to an outdoor café somewhat near the bookstore. As he was seated he saw her coming across the parking lot towards him and (almost thoughtlessly) gestured; she approached and he, emboldened by the circumstance, invited her to join him. She took the chair opposite: she had seen him in the book store! Wasn't he a Professor at the university? She had attended for a semester a year before, and recalled seeing him on the campus. Secretly, she always perused whatever volumes she had seen him reading at the bookstore: she was planning on returning to school someday! (He was embarrassed by this admission, recalling that he rarely chose a book of particular interest, but rather held one so that he might not be seen watching her…)

But what did he think of this-or-that author? And what of this-or-that book? He found himself answering and listening dreamily, distractedly, marveling at her comments as though glimpsing through a veil some long-lost home country, thought gone forever, come unexpectedly back into view…

(A sudden wind arose, blowing the table's contents into disarray, the stream of the conversation halted; in the lull he checked his watch and discovered that almost two hours had elapsed since she took the chair opposite his own. Impossible! Where had the time gone? (And what had they talked about? He could hardly recollect: the entire encounter lingered only vaguely, like a dream remembered upon waking, containing only impressions and no details, disappearing as it was recalled…) Standing he excused himself (the check had long since been paid), explained that he had a class to teach, expressed his enjoyment of the conversation they had shared, proffered his intention to continue the same again at a later date; she (standing too) enfolded him in a familiar embrace, echoed his sentiment, declared her anticipation…

That evening he argued with his wife (her son had refused to travel with her to pick up her niece) and (as had become customary when they fought) drove back to the campus to sleep in his office. Those students that remained from the walkout and subsequent protest rally were building a bonfire on the lawn; he stood with them until the police arrived and ordered them to disperse. He slept poorly (the couch in his office was too short for his frame) and, returning home the following evening, became rapidly annoyed when his wife apologized and embraced him (his back hurt from sleeping on the couch, and her additional weight was a burdensome and unnecessary discomfort). He could not, however, express this annoyance: to do so would be to engender future conflict, further travail; he instead resigned himself to standing, listlessly returning her embrace.

Soon his annoyance gave way to spite: why did she find it necessary to perform such dramatics? How ridiculous she was! Pressed to him she seemed a laughable and inferior creature. Harboring this secret hatred he excused himself (she raised her face and he bent obediently to kiss her) and explained that he had papers to grade, and so would be late coming home the following evening (this long-familiar excuse elicited only the most cursory acknowledgement).

The following evening he met the girl as the bookshop was closing. They went out to dinner and the next week did the same, and afterwards (with a boldness to which he was unaccustomed but whose near-frantic excitement he read as rectitude) he suggested that they go back to her apartment.

Once inside they moved together through an unbroken series of gestures and responses, and it was only in the quiet afterwards that it occurred to him exactly what he was doing, and what he had already done.

# CANTO THREE § CORDELIA

# 1

I have said that there is an Artist within me, and a Savior and Devil too; certainly you cannot understand what it is to be thus torn, to be haunted by your own mocking voice, its echoing and ever-pursuing laughter inescapable… No, you cannot comprehend that hell!

I have already described those moments (those delicious moments!) when I stood before a council of my father's friends, when this-or-that teacher praised me; I have already stated what it was to have that which lay at the essence of my alienation (my ceaseless scribbling, my ravenous and disquiet mind) declared the stain of genius. Perhaps it is laughable: perhaps you are right to laugh! Yet I cannot alter the fact: such comprised my sole point of pride, stood as the solitary column of my self-worth, upon whose single declaration I balanced the entirety of my young existence…

And yet it so often happened that this pride would collapse; my clever phrases and declarations – my proud Artist's stance (the mark and cause of my exile!) – stared back at me as though unmasked: divested of their transcendent quality (my pages comprised a laughable and misguided attempt, a ridiculous farce!), and I would sink into a despair from which neither praise nor rebuke could rouse me.

But whose voice declared my pages laughable? None but my own! My own bedeviled (and bedeviling!) brain produced these thoughts; my own lips uttered them! Why? And to what end? I can only return again to the nature of my mind, my ceaseless and consuming thoughts…

(Of what low intellect my supporters seemed at those moments! Sullied with wine they praised my stories; of what worth was their applause? Certainly little: certainly none at all! Perhaps you will be surprised to learn how dearly this revelation pained me; can you fathom that isolation? The fact of their negated praise seemed to disallow the possibility of any sympathetic ear, any compatriot soul…)

What precipitated this collapse? At times I beheld that my own rigorous criterion, my self-directing and self-denying principles had become yet another dogma in a world already overrun, and art another religion: yes, I had forgone their ordered Sunday universe only to find myself ever-encircled by a framework more rigid and more exacting, from which one received no comfort and within which one discovered no absolution. Likewise it was a framework resting upon human ignorance: did I imagine that I was wiser, more enlightened then they who sat in the Sunday pews, imagine that I could discern the universe's elusive truth, touch beyond the veil? Yes: I was forced to admit that such was my secret faith! And, like all faith, how laughable: removed from the ether and mingled with the dirt my proud and self-contained (and self-exalted!) rituals and offerings (my vigil before my writing table, my ramblings!) failed to inspire my heart from its stupor…

And yet there was Savior within me as well! For within this lethargy my mind always seized upon some idea, some seemingly profound inspiration whose intoxication was sufficient to rouse me, to silence the lingering voice of the Devil, to return me again to my faith and vigil… How ridiculous and exhausting this cycle; how laughable, when I see it thus dissected before me! Yet I can no more escape it than I can my own life…

## 2

And so it is only natural that again the Devil should strike! Sequestered in my garret I became convinced that the promise of my youth had come to fruition: that I had produced something of some intrinsic worth (the ethereal embrace seemed ever-nearer); I clutched the manuscript to my breast; for seven days the sight of those pages intoxicated me; I blinded myself to all doubt and pinned my hopes on their promise. And yet you already discern what followed: you have already discerned that happiness fits me poorly! On the eighth day I began reading, and my happiness collapsed: my insights devolved into rhetoric; what I took for subtlety seemed, at second glance, artless and obvious; my tirelessly deconstructing thoughts turned their attention back upon the works of their hands and found nothing redeeming there; the pages (and the months I had exhausted in writing them!) seemed an irredeemable loss.

The profundity of my impetus seemed entirely lacking from the tableau: Costard's trials satisfied me only in the most cursory way. What could I do? I was wracked with self-doubt, tormented by a sense of inescapable inadequacy; my efforts had garnered me nothing!

Yes; I was beset by nerves, wracked with despair: my months of effort had produced a work as bereft as all the foreign shores upon which I had stood and all of the ancient civilizations whose remains I had overlooked! A poor cast, enacting meaningless action upon a barren stage; a ridiculous sublimation, seeking an indefinite end; how ugly – how worthless! - my pages seemed to me then! With the final chapter closed I sank into despair: the fruitless hours that lay before me (no further effort seemed capable of achieving any greater success!) comprised a prison sentence, a condemnation from which I could not discern the method of my reprieve (but from which, I imagined, reprieve might be granted, were I but clever enough to realize it!); for three days I lay upon my cot, slept and woke beneath the hanging firmament of (what seemed to me then) the furthest limit, which no future effort could hope to surmount.

Thus to my Cordelia, my tormentor and my light, my critic and my muse: if not for her, these pages would be lost, burned, destroyed! For, despairing at my failure (the ethereal embrace was now denied!), I kept evening vigil at a tavern situated down the hill from my rented room; one evening (perhaps a week - perhaps two or more! – after that cursed eighth day, on which my endeavor's disappointment was revealed) it began to rain; I had no umbrella, and so I lingered in my chair past my accustomed hour; shortly after the barman rang the closing bell she came in: she had no coat, her dress was soaked through at the shoulders; she sat in the chair opposite my own and wrung rainwater from the material clinging to her calves. Soon she began to shiver, I offered her my coat; the room was crowded and too noisy for any other exchange…

Presently the barman corked the bottles, the patrons began their exodus (yet I hardly noticed; was it the wine that so intoxicated me? It is the natural explanation, yet I must insist that the sensation was unlike any wine stupor I had known: my thoughts and vision - my tongue in speaking – were clear!); the barman, preoccupied with his final tasks, did not disturb us; presently the rain lessened, and we walked out into the open air beneath dispersing clouds and soon-revealed stars…

## 3

But this is only a prelude to what so astounded me in what followed: I repeat that the tavern was crowded and too noisy to speak; when the patrons began their exodus I remained taciturn, offering only simple questions and no explanation of myself (this reticence continued after we had made our exit; she knew only my name, the nature and location of my lodgings, and the brief explanation that I had been traveling for some time). She, however, spoke at length: she had come from a small gallery opening further down the river (upon which the town was situated) and been caught out in the rain (it only occurred to me later to wonder where it was that she was walking to); she walked with powerful and rapid steps such that I had to hurry beside her lest I fall behind and out of earshot (for she spoke verbosely, unapologetically following the twisting stream of her thoughts, referencing archaic symbols and ancient texts with little concern for any but her own understanding; these words I chased as though in a nightmare, unable to hurry fast enough!

But I have introduced her enough: I will let her speak!)

"… One cannot merely cast oneself upon the rocks and forgive oneself because one calls oneself Artist; suicide is an artless act! The neuroses that plague the Artist may sing the praises of the noose or the bullet; let them sing! I laugh at all Lazarus Artists, all would-be initiates! I say to them: cast yourself upon the rocky shores and I will laugh at the works of your hands, will declare them worthless and false! I care nothing for your stupor nor your despair! You are alive, the world exists: he who demands more is a fool!

"And your claims of an ever-following bedeviling voice taunting and devaluing all the works of your hands: I laugh at them as well! Yes, and the angelic voice within that lifts you from despair: your unholy trinity repulses me! You have only your one set of eyes: look out through them! The tigress does not imagine that she is three instead of one!

"There is more to art than your infantile yearning for maternal regard! There is more to art than this dissatisfaction! Art is not art if it celebrates all that the world is not! One should paint or sculpt as one makes love: joyfully, passionately, forgetting all awareness of oneself! Yes: art should be this blessed dissolution! The death-seeking Artist finds only his own face staring back at him: he is Narcissus, in love with his own reflection! But now we have arrived: it is here that I leave you!"

She had been speaking as though to herself, with little concern for my ability to stay abreast of her words: thus I was startled to realize that these last were directed at me. Looking up I saw that we had come to a junction, the road which we had followed forked: one branch led down toward the river, and disappeared through a dense stand of trees and brambles; the other followed the clearer path before us, and was met further on by a third leading away from the river and upwards, out of its valley.

"Your garret is that way," she said, indicating the direction from which we had come. "It is a far walk and I apologize for having drawn you so far afield. Nevertheless, it cannot be helped now; in any event it does not appear that the rain will return. Good-bye!"

"Wait!" I cried (she had already turned and begun to descend, but turned back and paused).

"Do not worry!" she said. "We will see each other presently. I know where you live, and may find you any time that I wish. But there is nothing more for us to say tonight; in any case I am raving, and apt to confess more than I should!" She turned and began again to descend; I watched until the hanging boughs obscured the road; she made no further gesture to indicate any thought of my presence there…

## 4

Have I convinced you of my despair? Have I adequately conveyed my sorrow such that you will understand the wonder of what followed? For I returned home (the stairs made me out of breath, the wine made a torrent in my blood), my manuscript lay upon my writing table; I was inspired to take pencil in hand: this must be cut, and this as well! And here: this too! And ah yes: this could be conveyed more correctly, stated in this other way!

(For how long did I maintain this exercise? I do not know: when morning overtook the night it likewise found me still seated at my table…)

I was again impassioned, inspired: my thoughts led easily to each other; I wanted for neither word nor metaphor. It seemed a miracle: my irredeemable months were redeemed; my pages were not lost! When I collapsed into exhausted sleep it was with joy in my heart, with certainty that the coming weeks would bring with them the fulfillment of that promise; I slept and dreamed of Cordelia (my inspiration, my vision!) as she appeared descending beneath the boughs…

Yes, and in the fevered days that followed that evening that I understood: I had called my *desideratum* an indefinite end, and yet ascribed it to Costard as though he alone would suffice! What could his struggle be but both precise and inaccurate (for Costard's attempt to recapture a nostalgic ideal holds nothing of my Artist's striving, offers no intimation of that seeking which led me to traverse the globe!); and what could I do but abandon him for others? (And in whom but an Artist could I capture my striving, my ethereal aspiration and failure? In whom but a Seeker could I articulate my misguided searching?)

Yes: I labored in near frenzy at my writing table (my hands shook as with fever; my previous despair seemed a distant memory): visions of Hermione, of Leontes, arose before me, portals to elusive Truth, beckoning me onward! (Others haunted by inarticulate dissatisfaction, through whom I might yet grasp my cherished *desideratum*, to whom I might ascribe equally inaccurate and yet differently specific yearning (and through whom I might yet achieve that ethereal regard…)

(How the Devil within me laughs at the memory of that impassioned self-assurance!)

# CANTO FOUR § THE ARTIST AND THE SEEKER

# 1

Here: here are those pages!

...In the morning (Leontes' kisses were not yet forgotten by her skin) she became repulsed by the sight of her own work: the off-color fruits and disproportionate nudes, the inhuman faces and the depthless landscapes, confronted her; the vague dissatisfaction produced by each, now taken together, spoke of undeniable failure. How worthless – how laughable! – her efforts! She had no more achieved her elusive goal than she could compel her heart to cease...

She considered the most recent: a man seated at an outdoor café held a glass between the table and his mouth, the woman sitting opposite dug in a deep-red purse, a group of waiters leaned against the fence, a dog barked towards the street; each decision rested on another (the way the man was facing had made her think that the dog should be barking, the dog barking made her think that one of the waiters should turn); each was undercut by its arbitrary predecessor in a deconstructive chain leading back to the blank canvas. Her life (the move west, the city she had selected, the galleries she petitioned, the subjects she chose) had arisen in just this same way! Each decision rested on another which rested on another, resting on finally nothing save defenseless impulse and unjustifiable whim.

She felt a void opening before her, felt seduced by despair: it seemed that nothing remained save confession and attrition to the life she had forgone in the name of her artistic pursuits (the life she had called ignoble, bourgeois: a suburban life (like her sister's!)

growing fat and bored, aging meaninglessly into oblivion…

She opened one of the apartment's windows and climbed out: each floor made a ledge; she sat and watched the cars and people moving in the street a dozen floors below and let her feet hang in space…

(Yes: certainly you see something of my own despair in Hermione's crisis; doubtless you will recall that I, too, stood upon the precipice! And yet likewise you have discerned as well that such abstract crises (though keenly felt!) fail, at that crucial moment (when one tilts one's thoughts against the world and hangs on the brink of action!), to achieve their ends: how I rejoice and lament, to find my own calamity listed beside all those others whose dire consequence amounted only to theoretical speculation… How I mock my own inaction! (Yes: and mock my retreat, when in that void I sensed a nervous and excited possibility…)

But here: consider what follows!)

She thought suddenly of Leontes; what if he should wake, and see her? Imagining herself as he would see her she experienced a painful self-awareness from which she recoiled in disgust: how romantic she was being; how overdramatic!

She had imagined herself struggling nobly against the artifice that crept always into art, striving through falsehoods towards an elusive truth. But now: how laughable she was! Even her despair was only the performance of despair! Hadn't she hoped, after all, that he would see her, call out to her, regard her with newfound appreciation for the gravity of her plight?

She pulled her feet back from the edge. It was obvious why her paintings failed: each was irredeemably tainted by her artistic posturing! She climbed back through the window.

(Yes: Hermione is again myself! I contemplated various devices, stood upon the precipice and considered the storming sea, and yet at each (when that crucial moment arrived, when I felt my heart's beat nearing its climax!) I became repulsed, saw myself in the harshest light: the posturing Artist, the self-aggrandizing youth who imagines that his pain is deep and without balm! How the Devil within me laughed (and how his laughter pursued me, as I made my solitary way down amongst the rocks…)!

Yet at this the Artist too rears his head, contends that such is an Artist: that one must indulge oneself to achieve oneself; one must give oneself over fully to one's heart's violent beating; what dangerous time is youth to an Artist, when the heart's yet-unchecked impulses and reversals give rise to so many self-destructive possibilities: how earnestly I yearned to end my life! How it horrifies me now! Yet this horror, I am certain, acts as little deterrent to whatever impulses may in the future arise…)

## 2

She went down the hall and climbed into bed beside him; half-waking he curled into her arms and she was overcome by a sudden swell of emotion: she was holding life in her hands! The whole of her orchestrated being seemed woefully insubstantial when weighed against the certainty contained within this irrefutable sensation. It was suddenly clear: what she wanted was not a painting at all but a child; a child was like a painting that could not be false!

Yes: a child, arising from her inner self, would form then more perfectly an expression of her inexpressible interior! (For what was art, if not the struggle to translate one's inner world into the forms of the world at large? And what was a child, if not an inspiration rendered in flesh and bone? Yes: there was no greater art than life!)

She wanted a child, she roused him from sleep; three months later he awoke to the sound of her cries and a warm dampness beneath him. She clung to his arms in the ambulance, and yet following their return home she made little outward display of her grief: she fell almost immediately into a blank and impenetrable ambivalence. What could he do for her? She replied that she wanted nothing from him.

They had met at a party, she had invited him upstairs to see her paintings; in the morning he explained that he was on the road, and in the wordless exchange that followed it seemed established that he would stay with her. Soon two months had passed, then three and four: they fell into an effortless orbit whose ease comprised, they were equally certain, a profound sign indicating the rectitude of their union. Each had discovered its soul's complement in the other! Yet finding now that he could do nothing to comfort her (that she would not allow his comfort) he felt, for the first time, an unwelcome presence: all that had come before seemed lost behind the boundary of the evening when her cries woke him; he left and went to India, where he sat at the feet of great mystics. Life was like a waking dream, they told him; to die was a great blessing. To live was to desire, to desire was to suffer; even the most devout aesthetic was tempted! The world sang an alluring song, but its claims were false! Only the middle way led to peace and ripe wisdom.

It was only right that they had lost their child; all flesh grew old: the way of the world was loss! They directed his attention to the walls, where each week were posted pictures of the newly dead…

# 3

Imagining a partner for my Artist I imagined one to whom I might allot my forgone searching impulse, my belief that the unexplored world held some elixir, and in so doing cast it finally from me: having found no reflection of myself, no compatriot spirit, my previous searching seemed naïve, ridiculous; I laughed cruelly at myself in memory, and declared my difference!

Yes: I am the Seeker that the Devil mocks, imagining always that some elusive union of place and heartbeat, of reverence and earnest effort might enact some palliative transformation! Did I imagine that the relentless course of my ever-pursuing and dismantling thoughts would cease if I merely observed the sunrise over this-or-that temple, across this-or-that desert? Did I truly believe that I would lose the Devil's ever-mocking voice by pressing farther into the jungles, by traversing further into the ocean, by traveling deeper into the earth? Yes: I truly believed! (And did I believe, also, that in these multifarious and strange climes I might discover some indefinable and half-imagined truth, some oceanic feeling to erase the scars of all my lonely years… Yes; yes, I believed! How laughable it now seems!)

So you understand now that to me Leontes comprises a comic figure, a grotesque self-portrait: you will understand also then the wonder of what follows! For my Cordelia, upon our subsequent encounter (arriving at my usual hour I found her seated in my accustomed chair, read in her look an invitation) expressed interest in my ramblings; hurrying home I returned with the manuscript again clutched to my breast, and laid it before her; she called for more wine; I sat in silent anticipation as one page folded onto the next, her eyes never rising from my words…

(You cannot imagine my anticipation! For recall my childhood daydream: my fantasy of the lost notebook, of absolution in another's understanding; imagine if you are able that long-deferred yearning, now sighting again its aim!)

And imagine my joy when my Cordelia praised my work, and Leontes above all others; how dearly I cherish the memory! And how my heart trembled at the thought of that previously shameful inborn link between us: her words fell upon me as a sacrament, an anointing oil, a baptismal stream! For it was those moments wherein Leontes most reflected myself that she chose to mark (his manic yearning and earnest searching are doubtless my own!); disregarding all others she expounded (as though attuned to my particular self-conscious anxiety!) on his virtue as both character and archetype. (Here: returning to memory I find each detail etched there: unwavering gaze, emotive gesture, hypnotic motion of lips giving voice to blessed thoughts; how my own hands trembled, heart gave way to violent beating! Here: here are her words!)

"The Seeker need not be ashamed of his seeking! For there is nothing in this world but to seek and, when seeking fails, seek again! For where is the near boundary of heaven? Beyond where is the ethereal plane glimpsed? Nowhere or somewhere: it is one or the other! Yes, I praise your Seeker, would that I had the strength to be like him! More than all others I empathize with his plight! For one never knows what it is within which one struggles; one must either seek to know or else settle beneath its heavy yoke, its abstruse toil!"

(My soul leapt at these words, and yet my heart trembled too with fear! For her praise beckoned me further towards my own self-encircling thoughts, beckoned me indeed further from the world…)

But here, the Devil will not be satisfied, accuses me now of presenting my flawed self only through screens, presenting first the praise so as to incline you towards praise yourself! Here, he insists: show them! Show them how laughable you are!

He awoke on his cot, he left his room; passing through the entryway he caught sight of his own reflection in the window glass and, for a moment, did not recognize his own face. (Had he dismantled his self, moved beyond the forms of the world, become enlightened? No; he had not seen his own reflection for a number of weeks (his hair had grown longer, his beard had grown in, his skin was brown from the dirt and sun); these combined produced a (fleeting) unfamiliarity.) He realized immediately (and with disappointment) that this lack of recognition indicated no spiritual growth: the displacement, after all, had carried with it no sense that he was floating free, cut loose from familiar things…

Or had he felt cut loose from familiar things? He could not be sure; perhaps he had! Considering the possibility (that he had inadvertently experienced a great truth) he could hardly contain his excitement: he went to tell his guru.

But his guru was deep in meditation: he sat down outside the door to wait. Soon some of the other Americans walked by, and one of the girls stopped to talk to him. What was he doing? He was waiting to speak with his guru; that morning he awoke and, catching sight of his reflection in the window glass, had failed to recognize his own face. The girl was impressed, and the other Americans nodded their approval; they all agreed that he was making great progress.

The girl agreed: sometimes she thought she wasn't getting it at all! Her mind wandered all the time when she was meditating; she could not even focus on her mantra! How did he do it? She did not think she would ever get to the point where, upon waking, she would look into the window glass and fail to recognize her own face.

But she thought that it was easier for men! A girl put all of her heart into watching her own face; from her twelfth birthday she kept an agonizing vigil at the bedside of her own appearance. She was always over-aware of her body as herself; men looked at her, her mother looked at her, she looked at herself, always equating the value of the person inside with the characteristics of her external appearance!

The other Americans nodded and shrugged; perhaps it was their karma!

Would he walk with them? His guru was still motionless, sitting with his back to the door; Leontes rose and went with them. They walked past the pictures of the newly dead and through the garden where the monks were tending the flowers and then down the road into the market. The girl who had stopped to speak with him clutched his arm; wasn't it intoxicating? And had he ever seen such colors? And the people, animals, smells, sounds: it was all too much! Should they all separate and meet up later? It was madness, trying to stay together in the crowd! Why didn't they meet back at the foot of the hill, when the monks rang the supper bell? She took his hand and they moved off together from the group.

What did he think of this? What did he think of these? Oh, her mother would just love this skirt; her sister would adore these earrings! Oh but she could kill someone for a cigarette! Should they go find some? Did he mind? She took his hand and they continued deeper into the market.

Didn't he just love this town? Just look at the buildings! (He agreed that it was a beautiful town; he shooed away the children that thronged them.) And look at this little hotel; could they go inside? They went inside; a woman smiled at them from behind the desk; did they want a room? The girl went to speak to the woman, he could not hear them over the noise from the market outside the door…

Then the girl returned and took his hand: she led him up a narrow staircase and down a hall; she produced a key and opened a door. They went inside and the girl pressed her mouth to his. Afterwards they lay on top of the sheets in the too-hot room with the sounds of the market outside the pane-less window and she asked did he think it was wrong? Was it a betrayal of all that they had come to the monastery to pursue? Were they weak? She had heard about the child he had lost: there was so much sadness in him: so much beautiful sadness! She had wanted that beauty to become part of her; was it wrong?

He said that he did not know.

But she could kill someone for a cigarette! And there was still so much to see! They dressed and descended the stairs. Later they sat beneath a tree by the river smoking and the girl said there was too much beauty in the world to deny herself anything, that she was in the wrong place, that she could not believe in any truth that came as a reward for retreat from life. She held his hand; the market was loud and colorful and bright through the trees behind them and before them lay the slow brown river, and he was reminded of something he could neither articulate nor fully recall...

The girl left two days later; a week after that he awoke with an urgent nostalgia, an acute homesickness that was, he decided, a powerful love for Hermione. He stood before the pictures of the newly dead and wept as the monks shuffled past him into the garden. It was all so sad, so unbearably sad! Perhaps he was weak; he did not care! He fell to his knees, and from there collapsed onto the floor. One of the monks called to two others, and the three carried him, limp, from the hall into a darkened room and placed him on a palette. One of them pressed a cool compress to his head; one of the others left and returned with the abbot.

The monks spoke to the abbot, but Leontes could not understand what they were saying. He slept and woke some hours later, when a monk brought him supper. But he was only able to eat a little, and soon fell asleep again. He was awakened sometime later by the arrival of an English-speaking Indian doctor who told him that he was very sick.

What was it? Oh, it was nothing that he had not seen before. Although - he laughed - he had never seen it here! The doctor winked at him. But he would prescribe a course of treatments that, with luck, would eradicate the problem. In the meantime he would likely be very weak, and should be sure to get plenty of rest. He would leave instructions with the abbot, and leave it to his discretion; after all, it might make it difficult for Leontes if the story got around! The doctor was preparing to leave; he would check back in a couple of days. But what was it? The doctor peered at him over his glasses and said that it would do him no good to ask questions, as he was in the throes of a serious fever. They would talk when he was more recovered.

(He felt certain that the doctor's doting manner would drive him mad; he made to rise up from the palette. He would grab the man by the collars, and shake the answer from him! Instead he found himself overcome by exhaustion; he fell back on the palate and from there fell into fitful sleep.)

For four days he was unable to wake from a dream in which he lay upon a sweat-soaked palette:

there was no day or night, only a constantly-shifting light pattern on the wall opposite and a hazy stream of bodies and faces coming and going, a processional of monks forming outside the door, waiting for their chance to come in and look at him. And he knew why; yes, he knew why! They were coming to look upon him as they looked upon the pictures of the newly dead, coming to stand in the presence of the weakness of the flesh! Yes: he had become their meditation, their lesson; through him they would continue onward towards enlightenment! (He wanted to reach out to them, to speak, to beg one of them to stay beside him. Their presence was such a comfort! But this desire produced no result; he could not so much as lift his hand, could not entreat his tongue to speak...)

It seemed to him that he was going to die; he was filled with a seemingly infinite sadness. A weak protest arose within him and then collapsed; he was so tired! He did not have even the strength to refuse to succumb. Oblivion came up as a great black wall like a sea swell, and for four days he lingered in its shadow.

On the fifth day the doctor returned and told him that he was looking much better. An insistent hand pressed his forehead, his cheeks, his neck. How did he feel? Much better, yes; the worst was over. No, no (the insistent hand pressed down on his chest); he should not try to sit up so soon! He must take his time; he was still very weak!

(He wanted nothing more than to push away the doctor's hand, to show the doctor how wrong he was! He was infuriated when, after only a minor and momentary effort, he was wholly spent and could only sink back onto the palette. The doctor smiled sweetly down at him, a frustrated sob broke from his lips;

mounting all of his effort he turned away from the doctor to face the gray stone wall.)

The next day he returned to his room, and in the evening attempted to walk in the garden. But even this minor exertion proved too much for him; one of the monks was forced to leave his duties and help him back to his room.

He felt as though he was a tolerated child among patient adults: adults who were content to wait until he grew tired of their company (as they knew he would) and retired to the familiar world of children and their games. Their benevolence towards him, he suspected, was that of the intelligent towards the stupid, the enlightened towards the worldly. Feeling increasingly slighted, he regarded them with bitterness; their demeanor towards him was an unbearable insult! (Once, out of frustration at their manner and his own weakness, he yelled at one of the monks: when this too was met with the same pleasant indifference he began to swear at them, to insult them. They could not understand him, perhaps; but surely his manner was unmistakable! But entrapped by lingering weakness he was likewise fixed by their benevolent gaze; they continued to smile, to nod, to tolerate his offenses.)

He complained of this to his guru, who smiled good-naturedly. Resentment was a negative emotion, one that reinforced a concept of the self as an autonomous being, separate from an antagonistic other: surely he did not think the monks were motivated by such a destructive impulse! Perhaps he should look to himself for the source of the problem: was it possible that he knew too well the cause of his illness, and felt that he had betrayed his own higher aspirations? It was only natural to displace such feelings outside of oneself!

But think: he had desired and suffered; such was the nature of life!

Would he stay with them, then? He indicated that he would not; the monk seemed saddened by his refusal. Of course: if that was what he felt he had to do! When the doctor declared him well enough to travel, the Abbot would arrange for a car. Leontes shook his head; he would not see that doctor again! The monk looked at him with alarm, but did not argue. He should see about a car right away, then? Leontes assured him that he could not do it soon enough.

The car arrived; one of the monks carried his bags while another walked close beside him. He got into the car; through the window he could see the garden and the few monks working. Then the dinner bell rang, and those monks and the monks that had assisted him went back inside.

The car started down the hill; the market was closing and the street was nearly empty. They crossed the bridge that spanned the river and Leontes felt a sudden panic that he would never return to this place again, and was being carried from it too swiftly. He searched the bank for the tree beneath which he and the girl had sat, but was unable to identify which one it was. Then the road passed over a rise, and the river sank beneath the horizon. He wanted to tell the driver to stop: it was of paramount importance that he look at that tree one last time! But he said nothing, and with each passing moment the town disappeared further into the distance behind them.

It took him three days to return: he telephoned from New York and when he arrived at her apartment he was pale and trembling and had not slept for thirty-six hours. He crawled into her bed and slept through the night and most of the next day. When he finally woke she fed him bread; later they walked through the park and he told her about the monks and the temple and the market, and how oblivion had swelled like the sea before him, and how he had spent four days lingering in its shadow…

## 4

But what of Hermione? What of my cherished Artist? Did I blight her with tragedy and then abandon her, just as my Seeker had? Certainly not! But what can one do for one afflicted with such sorrow? Nothing, certainly: one always faces one's sorrow alone!

How vaguely I recall (vaguely and yet vividly: memory is such a marvel as to join (like a dream!) intensity and subtlety, to visit significance upon the insignificant, to thrust to the forefront of importance that which remains partially realized!) months in my early years: my eldest sister had been married (I recall only glimpses of the ceremony, though I bore the ring!); soon after came an excitement hushed by modesty, a guarded explanation that soon there would be a child; how little I understood then! (And yet how clearly I remember my sense of previously unknown gravity; recall the profound hatred I bore the man who had entered our lives and enacted this change; how the memory of his face still elicits powerful and thoughtless response, even now after these years!) I, looking to my father's face, saw no expression which I (a mere child!) could decipher…

And then: an altered but equal gravity; the unmistakable sound of my sister's sobs (muffled by the walls and the pillow with which I enwrapped my ears, but unmistakable still!); and simply no more talk of a child; again, how little I understood! (And those bedclothes which my father, returning from his daughter's house, saw fit to burn behind our house; a destruction insufficient to wipe out the stain which lives yet in my memory: the glimpse of red amongst the white...!)

It was such to which I sought my reckoning! Yet I find now that no such reckoning has been enacted: that marital consecration is for me tinged with that horror whose presence I sensed but was kept from facing (that it is likewise some sublimation of the same that inspired Leontes' trial); yes, how the Devil within me laughs! How I laugh now (as I am certain my doctors and attendants laugh!) to see my neuroses so clearly displayed...

(Yes; and now perhaps you call me cruel to enact such unpleasant and unnecessary trials, to rain down hardships as God upon Job (as the various Gods upon Ulysses)! The Absurd Man laughs his scornful laugh, assures you that her sorrows are far from finished...)

But enough: my cherished Artist stands alone, or not at all!

> In his absence she fell into a progressless limbo of undefined waiting: it was futile to imagine a future with him until she was offered some certainty of his return, yet she could not help but dread this possibility for fear that, during his absence, whatever had been between them (owning such bizarre origins and progress, it was nothing if not indefinite!) had vanished. She was therefore torn between hoping for his return and wishing he would stay away forever, like a pendulum which, suspended between two extremes, is constantly in motion but makes no progress. She was overwhelmingly relieved when, returning with him to her apartment, he fell asleep and awoke only after the interval for an awkward reunion was past.

But as he told her about the daily prayers and the hard palette where he slept she felt distracted and uncomfortable; she longed for the time when his stories would be exhausted, when his attentions would return to the concerns of their life together. (The possibility that he could be both present and absent, both in her arms and gone, had never occurred to her.)

This longing manifested strangely: she felt again that she wanted a child. Would he make her pregnant? He embraced her: it was wonderful; he was so proud of her! Bolstered by his enthusiasm, she assured him that she was ready. They returned to her apartment: as he kissed her she became suddenly detached; she watched the progress as if from outside of herself. (She was surprised by her own behavior: she was so assertive; it was so unlike her! As though, by pressing her body to his, she could eradicate the time that had passed, could sever connection to her extended interval of meaningless waiting and inaction…)

Disparaging her former artistic aspirations her opinion of herself had become inexorably linked with the promise of who she would become through him: he was a part of a becoming whose progress had been suspended by his absence, which could only resume upon his return, which would end with their child's birth and a happiness more perfect than any she had ever known. Was she, then, lifted from her malaise, gratified by the ensuing pregnancy and birth? On the contrary: she spent the pregnancy in a nervous frenzy that changed but did not cease when the child was born.

(Having birthed the child she fell into fitful sleep, and awoke with a strange feeling of weight upon her chest. She was surprised to find the child slumbering there.)

What did it mean? That she was unfit to be a mother: there was no other explanation! Other women experienced euphoria; she experienced the birth only as a weight placed upon her chest!

The prospect of maintaining watchful care over the child suddenly confronted and overwhelmed her. The task of caring for the child - of raising her to adulthood - seemed an unendurable trial, one to which she was ill-suited and one in the course of which her true failings would be revealed (it seemed somehow that, as the child grew, she herself would lessen: that by the time the child was old enough to move away she would be no larger than the child was now)...

(Does such strike you as ridiculous? Remember! Hermione first conceived of a child as being like a painting which could not be false; when these indistinct fantasies gave way to more pragmatic concerns this primary sense of the child (as something arising from her inner self) did not lessen. When the child was born and placed upon her breast she was surprised by its unanticipated weight: suddenly confronted by the child's autonomy, it occurred to her that the child (having arisen from her inner self) could more accurately (and more effectively!) reveal her failings. Likewise the infant's cries produced a mild panic not out of concern for the child but out of fear that, in responding to them, she would reveal her own ineptitude. Should she do this, or should she do this other? She did not know (the child continued to cry, seemed content to taunt her with her incompetence); the jury of the world seemed always standing near, ready to condemn her for any misstep...)

She was met on the stairs by an elderly widow with whom she was familiar, who lived at the end of her hall, who had moved to the building against her will but at her children's insistence when her husband was killed in an automobile accident (which she often and loudly decried as a great tragedy but of which, it was common knowledge, he was the cause). Inquiring after the baby, the widow made a clucking sound with her tongue (the noise was intended to show adoration and sympathy; Hermione was, instead, repulsed): she heard the poor thing crying sometimes! But she knew some ways to comfort an upset baby: she could show Hermione the tricks she had used to put her sons to sleep, when they were being difficult! (The laughter that followed, Hermione knew, was intended to display compassion and camaraderie: instead, the sound made Hermione wince; explaining that she was in a hurry, she continued down the stairs.) Once outside she attempted to put the encounter from her mind. She found this to be impossible: the clucking sound the widow made echoed in her ears. How horrible! And that the infant had inspired the pretense for the exchange… She felt a sudden and irrefutable spite towards the child (which she immediately rejected but which, in fact, she failed to dissuade…)

Once, when Leontes was late coming home, she became convinced that she could not bear the sound of the infant's cries, and left the apartment: once outside she was at once relieved and horrified; what kind of person was she? How could she leave her child? She resolved to return at once. But she could not make herself; she walked to the corner where she encountered him on his return. What was she doing? Had she left the baby alone? He did not wait for her to answer; he rushed back with her on his heels.

The child was still crying when they arrived; he lifted her from the crib and cradled her against his chest. What had she been thinking, to leave their daughter alone! Did she see how upset she was? What could have possibly come over her?

The sight of them together produced in her a profound loneliness, and she burst into tears. Horrified by the distance she now felt towards them she sobbed that she did not know what was wrong with her, knew only that at the moment she left she had needed to be away from the child, far away! He continued to stare at her; she went down the hall and collapsed onto their bed. (The child's cries followed after her; there was no escaping the sound! She lay with her face buried in the sheets and listened while he attempted, in vain, to comfort their child...)

What could she do? She took a job and he stayed at home with the child. Between these two demands (the job and their daughter) she no longer had time to paint: arriving home one evening she found that he had moved all of her materials. She was at first angered and but then surprised when he explained that, as she had not used them in almost two years, he had assumed that she would not mind.

Had it been two years since she painted last? He must be mistaken! But he was not; he remembered very clearly the day during her pregnancy when, complaining that her growing belly had become an obstacle to her work, she had decided to leave off painting until after the child was born. And their daughter would be two in just a few months!

Had it been two years? A sort of panic arose within her: she had hoped that, as the child grew older, the feeling of terrible weight would lessen. Realizing instead that two years had passed with no change, it occurred to her that perhaps this feeling of weight would never lessen, that she would, in fact, feel this way forever.

And her options were so few! To commit herself to their child was to face a bleak future of endless reduction; to refuse was to face a boundless alienation (how he had stared at her, sheltering the child to his chest!). By occupying her days elsewhere she had managed to postpone the decision, but this was certainly no resolution!

Was it better to commit herself, or remain one apart? What should an artist do?

Dostoyevsky's Raskolnikov, having killed the old woman and her sister, was similarly overcome: having cleverly committed a crime and subsequently fallen victim to a heavy conscience, he found himself forced to choose between burdened freedom and relief in confession; finding the stakes impossibly high, he instead deferred to and retreated into the familiar veneer of life. Likewise Hermione rapidly dismissed the appearance of this profound dilemma, responded with light indifference: where did the time go? Soon their daughter would be off to school, and graduating before they knew it! She was growing up so fast! Perhaps it was time to start painting again! She rearranged her materials in an unused corner and set to work…

# CANTO FIVE § DAS INNERE AND DAS AUSSERE

# 1

And yet you see again that my allegories are inaccurate, inarticulate: you see again that my poor cast has failed to capture that which inspired their creation! (For where in Hermione's secret trial - in Leontes' fruitless searching - is Ulysses bound to the mast? Where is the song still audible from the distant *Sirenum scopuli*? And where are the man's glassy and transfixed gaze, the woman's silence: where is the Absurd Man opening his eyes? Where is that blessed blotting out of the meaningful matrix upon which the street, the buildings, the town, country, continent, race, rested; where is the inarticulate jumble of physical remnants? Where is that horrible freedom? Where is the barren promenade? Nowhere: I have failed!)

Yes: you see that I am inclined to regard this failure (just as my Artist, considering her paintings!) as my own, and assert again that my faith was misplaced in childhood years, when my father's friends praised whatever poor offering I laid before them: I was mistaken to trust in their words; I laugh again at my own immature self-regard! (For have I not explained with what irrepressible pride I stood before them? How laughable it seems! How laughable, when I find now my talents' poverty unequivocally revealed!)

And yet (the Savior within me protests!) perhaps one is always confronted thusly! One's interior defies expression: even the most articulate must admit that language, gesture, action fail to grasp completely that which inspired them! (Yes: art is more translation than alchemy; I offer no excuse! A man stood transfixed beneath a window; a woman, unaware, noiselessly sang; an arrow shot skyward felled a blackbird; bedclothes were surreptitiously burned: of what worth are these assembled and absurd *tableau* if not first instilled with my own insane ramblings, my bizarre exposition, my crazed explication? Divested of such they comprise a cryptic montage, and little else!)

But again you accuse me, saying, You have forgotten your characters, have usurped these pages; we care nothing for your rambling! Tell us what became of Leontes and Hermione! And what of their child? Or what, at least, of your blessed and treasured Cordelia? What of Costard? How the Artist within me laughs, declares his pride! For the question concerns no other but the main, and it is as well that I should appease you: Costard too found an impossible distance between himself and the world, found that his interior defied expression; Costard too felt himself forced to fashion his thoughts with dull and indelicate tools!

But here: consider what follows!

Hamlet, standing before Ophelia's grave, marveled at the body's progress from person to corpse to clay and found it wondrous that Caesar (who kept the world in awe), now returned to mud, might find use stopping a hole and keeping out the wind. Likewise Costard was confronted by the body's immutable progress: how undeniable was his body's existence in time! The graying hairs that crossed his chest and stomach, the fat that had begun to collect about his middle, the loosening skin across his elbows and knees all spoke of inevitable decline. Watching the girl touch him, he had the strange sensation that the body she was touching was not his own, but a stranger's.

Yes; he was not unlike Chekhov's Dmitri, noticing for the first time in the mirror that his hair had turned gray! He was growing undeniably older; life was passing him by! And soon enough he would succumb to life's endless forward march; what a prison the body was! One fell finally victim to its failure, and yet even while one was alive one was hampered always by its dull tools and paltry expressions! (For there were so many things he wished to express: so many things he had found himself unable to express! His heart was an ocean whose depths had not yet been sounded, and yet his body denied him articulate expression, threatened to end before his soliloquy was complete, or even begun…)

What profound horror! For his inner self gave rise to a hundred thousand thoughts and emotions that, left unexpressed, disappeared forever. It was like an obscure artist, working in solitude, whose work would be destroyed in the same misadventure that claimed his life.

This strange and sudden confrontation with his own body produced a nightmare in which his body was made of wood, and stood before a crowded lecture hall. A procession of soldiers entered; they formed a line between him and the students. The captain came in; he drew his sword and with the sword he signaled for the soldiers to aim. The soldiers raised their guns, the captain's sword tip wavered in the air; how beautiful it was, to die before his students! Costard raised his eyes to heaven.

The captain's arm began to tremble: the soldiers were waiting for the captain, but the captain seemed to be waiting as well. Then the captain sheathed his sword; the soldiers lowered their guns and filed out. Costard tried to call to them, but his wooden tongue would not work inside of his wooden mouth. Why didn't they fire? Had they seen that he was made of wood?

Mute, he watched them go. Only when they were gone did he notice that the lecture hall was empty; while he was waiting for them to fire, the students had filed out. Through the window he could see them gathering on the lawn.

There was nothing left to do; he began to gather his things. But he could not find his lecture notes; he was sure he had set them down on the desk when the soldiers came in. But now he could not find them anywhere. He searched the same places again and again. Had one of the soldiers taken them? Was it something in his notes that made the captain sheath his sword? He had the sense that, as the soldiers entered, he was just then approaching the handle of his argument. But he could not remember what it was, and now could not find the pages…

## 2

And here: here too!

…He dreamed that he was made of wood, his clothes were painted on; even his skin was painted the color of skin. He was giving a lecture to his class. He stopped; his wife and son had entered the room. His son held a carving chisel in his hand; without offering any explanation he approached and plunged the chisel into his father's side. A fine mist of sawdust fell from the place. The students looked down from their seats with expressions of amusement and disgust.

Costard pressed his hand over the hole; it made the sound of clattering wood. He felt sawdust falling through his fingers. A few of the students stood up and left. He continued on with the lecture. Students continued leaving until he was addressing an empty hall. When everyone was gone he left the building and walked outside. There was a dense forest surrounding the campus; the streets and buildings were gone and trees stood in their place. Sawdust was still trickling through his fingers, but entering the woods he felt suddenly at peace. What did it matter that they had not liked the lecture? What did it matter that his son had plunged the chisel into his side, with his wife smiling on? Nothing; these things mattered very little.

He came into a clearing, where an old man was sitting beside an open fire. The old man rose to meet him; Costard knew, suddenly, why he had come. The old man smiled. Costard climbed into the fire; the paint melted away; it was an incredible relief! He wept tears of gratitude. The branches swayed above him; beyond was the clear blue sky. He saw the rising smoke and knew that soon he would be rising with it, rising up towards heaven. He looked out into the clearing and saw his students; his wife and son were with them…

## 3

And here as well!

…He dreamed that his body was made of wood: he was a tree, standing in the forest. He felt the wind in his branches above; he felt his roots dig into the earth. Then men came out of the forest; one of them pointed to him and the others took axes and began to chop him down. It seemed to take a long time, but it did not hurt. Then he felt himself falling. Some of his branches broke and the men cut away the ones that had not. Then they tied ropes to him and dragged him from the forest.

Then more men came and together they stripped off his bark.

They cut him into two sections: one section was cut into planks and nailed onto a frame here he was mixed in with planks from other trees. When the hull was finished the men coated the inside with tar and pitch. Then they set his second section upright and hung a sail from its crosspiece.

They rolled the ship on logs to the shore. They filled it with provisions and then men climbed aboard and they traveled far out into the ocean. Soon they joined a fleet, sailing with many others. Then they landed and stayed for a long time. When they launched again they were separated from the other ships, and ran aground several times on various islands. Then Costard felt someone being bound to him; a man was being tied to the mast. A strange sound filled the air, and Costard felt the man pulling against him. But then the sound went away, and the other men came and untied the one that had been bound.

What was the sound? He was overcome with curiosity.

## 4

How earnestly I wished to express and be absolved, to reveal and find understanding! Yet my earnest efforts bore no fruit: proffering the beginning of this-or-that thought I found no spark of recognition to inspire me further; offering some sentiment I met only puzzled eyes and unapologetic dismissal. My heart beat with earnest yearning, begged an audience, received only mockery; what might I do but search for the face of merciful God in strange climes and upon rocky shores?

(And finding none there, resign myself to bitterness and self-loathing! For doubtless were my thoughts more perfectly expressed they would engender some response; certainly the failure was my own!)

But now you protest, saying "Was it not the praise of your father's friends that first prompted your insane scribbling? Certainly you cannot also claim that, standing before them, your thoughts were dismissed and disparaged: you have already told of their brandied praise!" Certainly you are correct; certainly my plight is of my own construction; certainly it is under my own direction that I live as though a wounded Artist, imprisoned within a pervasive and immutable misunderstanding! Yet I proffer in my defense that even amongst those bolstering voices I found no trace of understanding, nor credible sticking place to which I might bind my hope and upon which I might build some little self-regard…

And now I hear you laugh: you are correct to laugh! You who have suffered through my previous boasts are now asked to pity me in my self-loathing: ridiculous, absurd! Yet I maintain, in the least, that those sycophants who ringed my father and his wealth could no more dismiss my rambling readings than they could refuse my father's party invitations; their connections (through whom my stories began to appear in print) were offered in the hope of ingratiating themselves to my father, and indicated no true heartfelt affinity for the poor products of my hands.

Is it any wonder, then, that I would likewise condemn Costard to chronic and pervasive alienation? His interior experience, too, eluded eloquent external expression:

> How difficult it was to make his thoughts and feelings known! There remained an impossible distance between his words and his thoughts; others stared blankly back! (What profound horror! For his inner

self gave rise to a hundred thousand thoughts and emotions that, left unexpressed, disappeared forever…)

How he wished to stand before the captivated audience and reveal with eloquent prose the inarticulate jumble of his disjointed thoughts! Yes; his heart beat with no other wish! And yet observed by this audience he was again within himself, again forced to translate amorphous and inarticulate insight into base language; his wooden tongue clattered against his wooden teeth! Such bitter imprisonment! For that which ached within his heart to be expressed and absolved would wither and go unheard; the paper-thin veil that surrounded him would remain unbreached; he would remain always an island unto himself, an unknown country!

## 5

And yet soon again I realized my failure, saw again that Costard alone would not suffice! For how often had my self-loathing turned and become instead scornful pride; how often had I championed my failure and declared that the world was instead to blame? And where in Costard's dreams is that horror that the world remains - despite all earnest yearning! - cold, barren, unresponsive? Costard's dreams, after all, pertain to flaws in his own composition, not in that of the world!

What could I do but abandon him for others? Thus I condemned his wife; yes, Costard's wife, too, was troubled by dreams of inappropriate transubstantiation! While Costard slept beside her:

She dreamed that the world had turned to stone: there was a terrible and continuous noise outside; she wrapped herself in the bed sheets and went to look for its source. The street outside was filled with people: their movements were awkward; each step seemed to require great effort. She watched a man and woman embrace; the sound of their bodies coming together was the noise she had heard. When they parted a shower of rubble fell; their bodies had been damaged by the embrace. The man turned and she saw that part of his face was broken away; underneath was the same gray stone as the streets and buildings.

Then the man saw her; he started towards her, his arms open to embrace her. In a panic, she turned and ran from him. The sound of crashing bodies became punctuated by the sound of his heavy footsteps on the road behind her. She went inside an open door and up a flight of stairs. The hall at the top was lined with doorways; the doors were made of stone. She tried one, and then another. The knobs turned, but the doors were too heavy for her to move.

She could hear his footsteps in the stairwell; she tried another door. This one opened, and she fell inside. Standing up she saw that she was in a bedroom; she knew that she had intended to lead him there, that there she would surrender to him. She did not know why she had run from him, only that she was tired of running. It seemed silly to run; there was no point in running! She climbed up on the bed; he came through the doorway. As he lowered himself onto her she heard the familiar sound and knew that she was stone as well: felt the weight of her arms and legs and of her body made of stone. How strange it was! But in the dream she was certain that it was not strange…

# 6

And here as well:

She dreamed that the world was made of stone; everything was hard and barren and there was no place to seek shelter or relief. When she found herself in a world of stone she sank to her knees and sobbed; her sorrow seemed endless and overwhelmed her.

After a long time she heard riders approaching, and in her sorrow she prostrated herself upon the ground in their path. The riders drew closer; she could feel the horse's pounding hoof beats vibrating through the rock on which she lay. The rhythm of the vibrations comforted her and she wept with gratitude that now, at the end, God had sent death within a comforting messenger. They drew close and she closed her eyes; her only regret was that she would not have a chance to thank the men who were to deliver her heart's greatest desire. Then the hoof beats were upon her and her cheeks were wet with a fresh burst of tears: there was no pain; how great God was!

But then the hoof beats slowed; above and around her she heard horses breathing. She opened her eyes; the riders had drawn the horses into a broad circle around her. One of the men came forward and offered her his hand; she stood and allowed herself to be pulled up onto the saddle with him. Then there was a rush of speed and she was inside the thunder of hooves. Her tears dried in the wind.

They rode for what seemed like a very long time. Then a fire appeared on the horizon: they rode towards it; as they drew close she saw a camp sheltered by cliffs. Tents of heavy black material stood in a ring around the fire.

More men came to meet the riders. They showed her to a tent; a wide bed stood behind the central pole. The man signaled to the bed and she lay down upon it. She was tired from riding but when she got into bed she could not sleep. Someone started playing music; soon the men began singing. She sat up in bed; the men sounded very cheerful and she wanted to go and be among them. But then a man came in; he climbed into bed with her. When he was finished another man came in. Another followed him. Whenever one went in or out she could see through the lifted flap a line of men waiting outside. She was concerned that, if it took too long, she would miss the music going on outside. She wanted very much to see whomever was playing, to see the men gathered together and singing. But when the next man came in she saw that the men in line were singing, and the ones with the instruments was there as well.

She realized that she was the center; she had been alone and lost in a barren rocky expanse, but now the world gathered around her! The next man entered and she rose to embrace him. More men joined the first. Soon she was enclosed in the shelter of their bodies. Their weight was like the weight of the ocean above and around her. How wonderful it was, this feeling! How safe and carefree! She felt herself drifting off to sleep.

But suddenly she was sick at heart: she remembered Costard! How had she forgotten him all of this time? Her heart ached with earnest prayer that the night be erased. But it was done; how could it be undone? It could not be undone! It was an unbearable sin; a permanent stain!

One of the men's castoff belts lay upon the nightstand, a sheathed dagger still hanging from it. She clasped the handle; how the sight of her own hand disgusted her! The men did not stir; she unsheathed the dagger and plunged it into her heart.

# 7

And here!

She dreamed that the world was made of stone; everything was hard and barren and a cold wind blew across the flat open spaces. She was standing alone on an endless field of rock. She knew that her house was somewhere beyond the field. She picked a direction and started walking. After a hundred steps she turned around and came back. She started off in another direction, then turned around and came back. She did this many more times. She did not see anything; everything was the same flat open field of rock.

It felt as though she would never find her home; she sat down and wept. How pleasant home would be! She thought of the familiar corner on which it sat, the green lawn, the shady porch. Every memory of it filled her with perfect happiness. She saw herself going up the back steps and through the door; someone was singing upstairs and she followed the sound. The door to her bedroom was closed and she could hear that the singing was coming from inside.

She tried the door; it did not open. The singing changed, taunting her. Angry, she threw her shoulder into the door. She thought of demanding that the door be opened: after all, it was her house! But as she opened her mouth to speak it struck her that this was not her house.

Everything that had seemed familiar a moment before became strange. Of course this was not her house; the floor plan was completely different! Why hadn't she noticed that the staircase was in a different place, that the door she leaned against was not her own?

She heard the front door open and close; Costard's voice called hello. Panicked, she ran down the stairs and out the back door.

The yard seemed strange; the corner on which the house sat was unfamiliar. Looking around, she saw that she was in a maze of houses. Every house sat on a corner behind a wide lawn. She began running, turning from side to side, searching for her house. She thought she saw it down at the end of the street, but as she grew closer she saw that it was not her house; the eaves were different. She saw another that looked like hers, but the porch railings were wrong. She ran faster and faster, until the passing houses were a blur of white shutters and dark stain. Something rose up in her path, too late for her to turn, and she fell forward onto the pavement. She stood up; she was in the open rock field. There were no more houses, only a yellow sky and the bright spot that she took to be the sun. She was tired and wanted to sleep; what did it matter anyway? She could walk for weeks in this desert and never escape!

She lay down on the rocks, inviting death to take her. It came in a long shadow, and only when it had covered her did she realize that this was not what she wanted. She opened her mouth to speak, but inside of the shadow she could not breathe. How horrible it was to die! Endless, black, breathless horror! A chasm opened beneath her feet; she was falling and reaching out and there was nothing to catch her or hold her and there seemed to be no end to the darkness.

She offered up a prayer to God; high above her the clouds parted. There was nothing beyond them but the bright spot of the sun in the yellow sky. She laughed. Then the chasm closed above her, and she continued falling in the darkness.

# CANTO SIX § THE STUDENT

# 1

Costard suggested that they return to her apartment; afterwards he hurried home with an explanation for his lateness, for his not having called. But standing before his wife his excuses sounded protesting, absurd: what had seemed reasonable on the drive home now seemed strange and fantastic. He cursed himself; he was such a fool! Had he really thought she would believe him? She would see through him; she always saw through him! If she probed his explanation, he was certain, he would fall to his knees and confess.

But his wife was busy, and seemed to be neither paying attention nor concerned. He had been where? Of course: and how was this-or-that colleague? She kissed his cheek; she would be up in a bit; she had a few things to finish up. He did not have to explain himself! Had he thought she would suspect him of something illicit? She laughed; she knew him too well to imagine that! (This last, he knew, was not a proclamation of her confidence but an estimation of his prowess.)

Raskolnikov, hearing that the only man aware of his guilt had shot himself, was overtaken by giddiness and left the police station. It was the same with Costard; convinced that his wife would (somehow) detect his infidelity, he had returned home as one climbing the steps to the gallows. When she scoffed at his excuses and told him there was no need to explain himself, it was as though he had been granted an unexpected reprieve. His head swam, he reached out to steady himself; he left the room and went upstairs. In the closeness of the stairway he could smell her and was again overcome by a trembling euphoria. Had it really been her? Could it possibly have happened?

And that his wife suspected nothing, thought him incapable; how fitting, that her disparagement now blinded her to his infidelity! His heart filled with spiteful triumph which overwhelmed whatever lingering hesitation remained. He went to see the girl at lunch the following day, and on each of the three days after, and twice a week for the following two weeks.

## 2

By asserting the arbitrary nature of his life's composition Costard silenced his initial hesitations (what did it matter if he slept with the girl? And why shouldn't he? The universe, in its reticence, offered no compelling counter argument); consequently he pursued the girl on the (declared) precondition that he was essentially free to do so. Later this freedom (the universe's silence, his wife's ignorance) produced a startling effect: burdened by his secret knowledge, he began to entertain private fantasies of tearful confession and difficult attrition.

What was this fantasy? Standing beneath the window (the girl noiselessly singing) the defining confines of his life (familiar questions, demands, expectations) seemed both divested of authority (resting always on an all-surrounding void, owning no essential mandate, their self-appointed significance evaporated) and self-contained; it stood autonomous within an unexplored potentiality whose various possibilities (why not this life? And why not this other?) this absurdity allowed (to which his own life, having lost its previous and presupposed power to forbid, could now only voice its meager and ignored protestations). After he had slept with the girl (and thus begun a course whose revelation would dismantle the existence that had defined him for the preceding two decades) he imagined himself suspended between two worlds, each guarded by a woman. Thus mired in vague limbo (and having disregarded the intervention of any pertinent ideology) he (privately) yearned for the reassertion of some essential boundary.

What becomes of Ahab when God does not respond, when Heaven remains silent? Filled with a profound uncertainty (which course was the right one? And by what standard? The criteria set forth by his own familiar existence seemed hopelessly insubstantial!) he entertained fantasies of tearful confession and painful attrition.

## 3

(What is left for Ahab, when God does not reply? I traversed ancient ruins, stood upon foreign shores; I observed rare monstrosities and absurd cultures in the sad hope that some new effort might earn me acknowledgment from the reticent universe. How ridiculous, this searching! For I see now that every man builds his life as a tower reaching toward heaven, praying he will reach the distant beyond or be sent crashing to earth by some divine hand… How absurd, when in the end he goes on building, endlessly building, amassing only life onto life…)

# 4

Owning such disorienting origins, it was not long before Costard came to feel that he loved the girl, that he could not live without her, that she was the only good thing in his life. His wife did not understand him, students did not appreciate him, as she did; it had been years since he felt so inspired! (Yes: his inarticulate thoughts seemed ever-clearer; the ease and quality of his insights surprised him! As though, in some way, the girl held the key to a realm of understanding, an oasis of the spirit within which his ever-storming thoughts grew calm and into which he had been granted brief and blessed entry…)

Yes, certainly he loved her!

(But what was the nature of the love he imagined he felt? To what did it owe its origin? Her appearance, her manner, her having sung behind glass? No: love was the name given to the feeling he did not understand, the combination of affection and desire infused with the urgency of the transgression and sickled o'er by the hazy and irrational dream-cast of fantasy! It was the assertion of an essential boundary within which he was hopelessly kept and against which he could not fight (and thus would not try). In short, he declared his love so that he might forgo any uncertainty, so that the course might define itself; he professed his love for her with exactly the same relief in his heart as what he imagined would come should he fall down on his knees before his wife, offering tearful confession and painful attrition.)

His certainty regarding the love he bore her was punctuated by (rare) moments of (profound) clarity within which he felt his transgression as transgression, felt overwhelmed by guilt, felt the full gravity of his betrayal. In these instances his assertion of the relationship's transcendent quality (she was the gatekeeper to an oasis of the spirit!) seemed utterly laughable and his love hopelessly petty and juvenile: had he really imagined that he loved the girl? How ridiculous! They had so little to say to each other; she was discouragingly immature!

(Yes: his insights, though more eloquently articulated, failed to elicit comparable response: she had not read this-or-that book, did not know this-or-that author; how often he was forced to repeat himself, to do her thinking for her!)

The tryst thus divested of magic he imagined himself, in these moments, as one condemned: his eventual discovery seemed inevitable, held the threat that he would lose everything (his wife would certainly leave him, his son would turn from him); he would be exiled from his own life: a second bachelorhood was a prison sentence! Tearful confession and painful attrition seemed powerless to halt or assuage his inevitable condemnation.

## 5

The night his wife and son went to meet her sister (they would spend the night at the motel, and return the following day with his wife's niece) he took the girl to his house; he was filled with spiteful triumph (certainly he had now refuted his wife's low estimation of his prowess!) as he lowered her onto the sheets; he awoke in the night and was unable to separate the two: love and spiteful triumph.

He had seen the girl every week throughout the semester and now saw her more often; he had felt certain that he loved her, that he could not live without her, that she was the only good thing in his life. Now he lay awake, considering: perhaps it was not love! Perhaps what he felt was only some combination of novelty and spite that disguised itself as love!

He rolled to face her, and tried to determine what it was, exactly, that the sight of her sleeping inspired within him. He found it impossible to decide. (Without love to justify his transgression (love was an essential boundary, a mandated course!) he again felt mired in vague limbo, uncertain how to proceed.)

Finally he concluded that it would be clear in the morning: yes, in the morning he would wake and, seeing her beside him, would be able to judge by his response his truest feelings. But when he woke in the morning he was startled to discover that the body next to his was not his wife's. He took a shower, and when he returned she was already up and dressed. (Coming upstairs in the dark their bed had seemed like any other bed: now of course he could see that it was not and could see that she knew it, too.)

He dropped her off outside her building, then went home and changed the sheets. Moving to his wife's side (her bureau stood beside the bed; its contents had long since become a mystery) a thought struck him: perhaps his wife, too, had a lover! (The idea, he had no doubt, was an absolute absurdity; nevertheless his thoughts seized upon the possibility, proclaimed it a revelation: yes, the distance he had felt, the foreign quality of her moods, her prolonged and unexplained absences all found their resolution in this discovery! Certainly it was reasonable to imagine that she held a similar dissatisfaction, felt misunderstood;

perhaps she too had met someone, had the feeling that her life was a spider's web carried on the empty air!)

He imagined her (as much out of curiosity as desire to rid himself of his lingering and persistent guilt) with several of the men they knew (this-or-that colleague, familiar store clerk, this-or-that neighbor); he imagined them together and imagined himself watching, his heart filled with benevolence. Forgiving her (theoretical) indiscretions he felt suddenly certain that he could never lose her, that exile from his own life was an impossibility; how could he become exiled, when even this betrayal was powerless to dismantle the familiar (comfortable, reassuring!) composition of his life? Simple: he could not! The love he felt (as he descended the stairs, the tainted sheets beneath his arm) was more powerful than any he had felt in years.

## 6

By smiling benevolently on the most powerful act she could take against him (disempowering her forceful betrayal) he made her weak, and in that weakness he was free to love her: imagining her with another man he felt closer to her than he had in years. The thought of the girl with another, inversely, wholly horrified him.

What was this horror? It was not the fear of betrayal: it was the fear that, if he was one in a series, he was necessarily inextricable from those aspects of his life that (to external eyes) defined him; unable to slip from his life (if he was her Professor lover then certainly he could not assert the insubstantiality of that role!) the affair ceased to hold the possibility of another life and instead became a sad and ridiculous rebellion enacted within the prison walls of his own inalterable existence.

His mind recoiled from this thought: of course she was only his; certainly he could live another life! But during their subsequent meeting he could only think of her coupling with another. Consequently he grew withdrawn and suspicious: where had she been during the previous week? And who with? (Startled, she began to recite the unremarkable litany of the week's activities, with an expression both surprised and wounded; feeling monstrous he stood relentless before her; her explanation went on and on; finally she finished; and now she was here with him! Feeling ridiculous (her week had included nothing to incite his suspicion) he grew rapidly annoyed; why couldn't he get the thought from his mind? How absurd, when after all it was he who spent his nights with another!)

This initial tension was followed by a now familiar progress; afterward they lay in bed and the breeze through the open window blew her hair across his face. He was unable to stop it; she lay (sleeping) on top of him, his arms enfolded beneath hers. He grew rapidly annoyed, yet felt unable to express his annoyance: having already been the cause of unnecessary strain (why had he asked where she had been for the previous week? The anxiety seemed ridiculous to him now!) he felt that to do so would only incite her (rightful) frustration. He resigned himself to laying passively beneath her. But soon he felt that her meager weight was suffocating him; further, the heat in the room was unbearable! Bolstering himself with indignation he moved from beneath her and went into the bathroom. Away from her his annoyance quickly dissipated. Returning he saw that she had rolled onto her stomach; he felt a sudden urge to lay on top of her, to cover and enclose her body with his own.

# 7

A week later one of Costard's colleagues threw a party; he became separated from his wife in the crowd and presently, feeling drunk and bored, he went upstairs to his colleague's bedroom where he closed the door (the party was loud downstairs) and called the girl. She answered; she missed him! When was she going to see him? Soon; he would come see her very soon! There was a noise in the background; someone called her name. Was there someone else there? No, it was nothing! Yes, she had some friends over; she could not talk now. She would see him soon? All right then: goodbye! There was the sound of muffled laughter; the line went quiet; Costard let the receiver fall away from his ear.

Someone downstairs laughed; laying on the bed (without the girl's voice to focus on the room began to spin) he had the vague but seemingly immitigable feeling that he could never go back down to the party, that he could not face any of them, that to do so comprised an insurmountable trial through which he could not hope to succeed. But then the disconnected telephone began beeping, and so he sat up and replaced the receiver. In the silence that followed he could not remember exactly what it was that he had been feeling, and so he wiped his eyes and left the bedroom.

The door leading off the hallway to the bathroom was open, the light had been left on; he caught sight of his reflection in the mirror. His face struck him as profoundly funny: it seemed somehow ridiculous that the person staring back at him was himself. He started laughing; his laughter joined with the laughter from the party downstairs. But then lost his balance and had to catch himself on the door frame. Steadying himself, he turned out the bathroom light. The reflection disappeared; he went back downstairs to find his wife and rejoin the party.

## 8

The next day (she opened the door and embraced him, they went into the bedroom and undressed, she pressed her mouth to his) he was suddenly and strangely repulsed; the tongue in his mouth seemed a horrible intrusion, the weight of her body was unbearable! Afterwards he could not look at her. She ran her fingers through his hair and he withdrew (almost imperceptibly; were her fingers not pressed against his scalp, she might not have noticed); what was wrong? Nothing; nothing was wrong! She looked at him strangely; what was it? He grew quickly irritated; why was she so insistent? He wished she would leave him alone! He felt suddenly tired and that he wanted to fall asleep and never wake up.

How ridiculous – how absurd and burdensome! - it all seemed! The body that pressed down on his, the drive to her apartment, Sunday laundry, the brief litany of excuses he offered for his absence, the weekly rotation of dinners: his life seemed a room whose windows looked out onto brick and mortar walls and whose doors opened onto barren deserts and wasted fields; it overwhelmed and exhausted him! He went into the bathroom and, fearing that his wife would taste the girl on his lips, brushed his teeth. He imagined that he might again come out to find her laying facedown on the sheets, and again feel the urge to lay on top of her, to cover her with his body. But when he returned she was sitting up, facing him with a strange, transfixed expression. He was momentarily taken aback; the girl, seeing this, burst into laughter; he should have seen the look on his face!

It occurred to him that the girl was, in fact, little more than a child.

## 9

He had to be going; he dressed and went to the door. He would call her later! She did not respond; he went out and closed the door behind him. On the stairs he checked his watch and saw that he was running late; he hurried down and across the street to his car.

What excuse would he give? And would she believe him? A thousand unpleasant possibilities arose before him. His heart began to race; he would be found out! He pulled away from the curb. Nearing the end of her block he saw someone he recognized: a boy who had been a student of his. He could not be sure at first; was it the same boy? But as he came closer it was obvious: there were the large, searching eyes, the tight mouth (even the same scarf, and now, in July)!

His own situation seemed suddenly ridiculous; yes, he laughed out loud! Here he was, panicked over his great and dramatic trials while this boy, were he to notice Costard, would regard him as nothing more than his Professor, a summation of laborious assignments:

would take for granted the impossibility of the sordid affair from which he had come. (Yes, how strange: the role that for the preceding months had defined the *précis* of his too-confining life now seemed the obscuring shroud with which his liaison might continue, undetected. It occurred to him then that, rather than lead a second bachelorhood, he might (for many years!) pursue a second life hidden within the framework of the original. This tertiary possibility enlivened and inspired him, he regretted his previous annoyance; his heart filled with love and laughter as the framework of his existence again became insubstantial.)

Yes, he laughed out loud! But then he caught sight of himself in the rearview mirror; spending his life with students, he had almost imagined himself one among them. But it now was obvious; he was growing older! His hair was showing strands of gray; his beard could not fully hide the lines that creased his cheeks.

Yes, he was just like Dmitri, in the story by Chekhov! He was growing older, yet imagined that the future held a new and perfect happiness; how laughable he was! And it occurred to him that in fact he and the girl were wholly unsuited to each other. The student was far better suited to the girl than himself! (Yes; there was an unguarded and earnest quality in their thinking that had both frustrated and fascinated him; how many times had he been forced to correct her missteps? Yes; certainly the student was better suited to the girl!)

And yet he had told her that he loved her, that she was the only thing good in his life; how ridiculous he was! Driving away he knew that he did not love her.

# 10

The student went up the stairs and walked inside; she rose from the bed and embraced him…

# CANTO SEVEN § "IT SEEMED INCREDIBLE THAT HER FAMILIAR BODY COULD BE SO PROFOUNDLY ALTERED..."

# 1

Each aspect rested on another; each was undercut by its arbitrary predecessor in a deconstructive chain leading back to the blank canvas, to defenseless impulse and unjustifiable whim. She felt seduced by despair, felt a void opening before her; what was this void? The apparition of suicide, the specter of her own death? No, it was the nothingness stretching forever beneath the seemingly concrete aspects of her existence, the eternal blank canvas upon which she had enacted her life (and to which she would eventually return).

Costard, perceiving this insubstantiality (his life was a spider's web, blown free of its frame) silenced his hesitations; what did it matter if he slept with the girl? And why shouldn't he? The universe, in its reticence, offered no compelling counter argument; he was free, essentially free! Hermione (her life was a painting, whose producing brushstrokes could be attributed to no essential mandate), inversely, felt essentially and impossibly bound: the reticent universe offered no alternative; her life stood opposite an endless void; she was caged, eternally caged! The appearance of nothingness (empty air) for Costard negated whatever confining command his life might assert upon him; conversely nothingness (the blank canvas) for Hermione negated herself (what was the painting of, if not of her?), and horrified her with the threat of dissolution.

This horror (she felt a void opening before her, felt seduced by despair) inspired the sudden certainty that she wanted a child; yes, a child refuted the apparition of insubstantiality! (A child required constant care and attention; a child was an essential mandate!) Preoccupied with pertinent concerns she was not troubled by the thought that each aspect of her life was undercut by its arbitrary predecessor. She became pregnant, miscarried, spent a period of timeless mourning, became pregnant again; her child was born, and four years passed in which she was untroubled by any anxiety that her life rested essentially on nothingness.

## 2

But one cannot sustain such effortful existence! One must close one's eyes at every moment to that truth which one cannot ignore. (How long may one wish blindness upon oneself before one must put out one's eyes?) Likewise she became again confronted:

> Riding her bicycle home from work one evening a passing car clipped her rear tire; she was knocked to the pavement; as a result of this accident her right ring finger was amputated above the first knuckle (having no memory of the accident, she later assumed that it had become somehow entangled in the bicycle's components as she fell, and too badly damaged to be repaired). Later, changing the bandage, she was struck not with a sense of loss but rather one of wonder: it seemed incredible that her familiar body could be so profoundly altered.
>
> What was this wonder? Her life had seemed somehow interminable; she could not imagine her own non-existence. How was it possible that one day she would cease to exist? (It could not be possible! Every sunrise and meal and breath subtly reaffirmed her belief that it would all go on forever.) The wonder, then, was that she existed in time: staring at the sad nub of her missing finger (the black stitches stood out against the red skin) she was confronted by her own temporal

existence. Yes, she was in time, she lived as a body: one day she would be dead!

Perceiving this, the preceding four years (characterized by a progressless limbo and an undefined waiting) seemed wasted ones: what horror that these years, now spent, would not be returned to her! (What had she done? And what was it worth? She had always wanted to travel! And there were so many other lives to live!)

It was as though Leontes and their daughter stood before the vast untravelled world, and for five years she had refused to look past them.

## 3

She left the apartment and took a walk, expecting the feeling to fade. Instead it grew stronger: she could not bring herself to return home! She walked to work and took an early shift she was not scheduled for. Afterwards she went out to dinner and saw a late movie. After this, having nowhere else to go, she went home.

Where had she been? He had been worried sick about her! Confronted, she burst into tears; she wanted her own life! He was her boundary and she hated him, hated herself for being bound! She could not pretend that she was happy! They were wrong for each other, she did not love him; she was not certain that she ever had!

## 4

They talked for several hours, but could think of no solution. What could they do? She could not ignore the feeling that there was a vast world that she was missing, that life was passing her by. She was an artist; she needed change, conflict, inspiration!

She wanted to travel; what if they took a trip? She dried her eyes: a trip? Yes, a trip could be just the thing to help her find her inspiration! After all, she had the vacation time saved up, they had their savings; she had been through a lot; she deserved a trip! Yes, it was just the thing! She would have to work her remaining shifts, of course. Would he make the arrangements? She had always wanted to see so many places! There was so much to see, so much wasted time to make up for!

Imagining the trip, she felt almost instantly better. This course of action seemed the correct one; the undertaking seemed to promise real progress. The experience would change her, show her truths she had not imagined; think of the people she would meet! (They were not finished but only stuck in a rut; of course it was only natural for her to feel as she felt! After all, who wouldn't feel trapped, stifled, hemmed in?) She was sorry that she said she did not love him; it was not true; her heart now swelled with love for him!

Weeping with relief, she embraced him.

## 5

They took a trip; they traveled for two days and then met her sister and nephew at a motel. Their daughter hugged her goodbye, but refused to release her father. They reassured her: they would see her again soon; it was only for a few short weeks! Their daughter, undeterred, cried and clung to him; he said that he did not feel right about leaving her in this state; they stayed the night at the motel. Alone in their own room she lost patience with him; it did not make any difference how long they stayed! The child was still going to make a scene when they left; there was no use dragging it out! And besides, they were losing valuable time! They had to stay on schedule if they were to see everything she wanted to see!

He, standing opposite her in the narrow room, countered: perhaps she did not care about their daughter, but he did; he refused to leave her in her current state!

And it occurred to her at once that the trip was a mistake, that she had naively imagined that by leaving home she would leave her dissatisfaction behind. But of course the problems had come with them; they could not escape who they were, nor change who they were to each other. (It seemed he would always be eyeing her coldly, sheltering the child to his breast; she would always be standing some distance from them!)

This was who they were; they could not fight it! No cosmetic alteration could change their fundamental failings. She began again to weep.

## 6

Why was she crying? She tried to explain; she felt like a stranger in her own home, an unwelcome presence! Did he know what it was to be lonely in the presence of those whose very existence was supposed to eliminate loneliness forever?

He scoffed; could she really blame him for the way she felt? It was her own doing! If she felt alienated from them, it was only because she had alienated herself; the feeling that she was an outcast was her own construction! He had done nothing to make her feel that way; he wanted nothing more than for them to be a family!

Oh, so it was her fault, then? She buried her face in her hands; her altered finger still felt strange against her face, and the thought of it filled her with an unintelligible sorrow and horror. It was no longer an indication of the possibility for profound change; now it was a reminder of her body's decay! Yes, her body which she had taken for granted, hated, sought to alter, defiled; now it was collapsing around her!

And it suddenly seemed that her life was a waste, such a profound waste! What had she done? Why had she stayed? Where was she going? What was she doing? She did not know! And now there was no time left to change, no chance to start again! This thought overwhelmed her, and she sobbed uncontrollably.

# 7

He fell back on the bed; what could he do? He did not know what to say to her! Did she want to go home? Did she want to tell her sister that they had changed their minds, collect their daughter, and depart? Was she giving up on the trip? Was she giving up on him? She shook her head; she did not know, she did not know!

He went to her and embraced her (she sobbed into his shoulder); over her shoulder he could see through the open door into the bathroom. The grout between the floor tiles had turned black, the wallpaper was beginning to pull away from the wall, the room smelled strongly of mold; as she wept into his shoulder he found that he could think of nothing else. It occurred to him suddenly that she had been trying to express herself, to explain her loneliness and need, while fighting the overwhelming stench of ruin and decay. This fact, more than anything, filled him with pity.

How strange! She had been asking for his pity for years (asking for it, yes: and refusing to accept it!), but it was only now that his heart was moved. Her ludicrous artistic posturing, her layered-on cynicism, her devout faithlessness all seemed suddenly small and petty and laughable; he had the sense that he had been charged with the care of some inferior creature, one at a loss in the world and incapable of negotiating it without his assistance.

## 8

Yes, she was like a child; she longed to be loved, held, embraced, sheltered, praised, doted on! The birth of their child had succeeded only in ousting her from her place at the center of the universe. How ridiculous she was; how wholly absurd!

From the bathroom doorway they moved to the bed; they lay close together and then moved apart. In the night she reached for him and when he responded her heart filled with love for him and their daughter. In the morning they kissed their daughter goodbye and headed south. Riding in the car beside him she knew that she was in love and if love was doomed then she was doomed with it, and its tragedy seemed inextricable from its beauty. Their hearts shared a truth that their minds could not fathom; their bodies spoke a secret language that had existed since the beginning of time! (Yes; it was the language Adam spoke to Eve before the fall, forbidden in the deserts east of Eden, but still whispered between them in the night; their love was one such as this!)

What an amazing life she had lived! So much heartache and tragedy and despair and wonder! She had already experienced so much, and was still so young. Everything was as it should be; how wonderful the coming years with them would be! Their past unhappiness seemed far distant. She was no longer afraid; it was just as Mary must have felt, visited in the night by the Archangel Gabriel! Yes, she was just like Mary: Mary who suffered the loss of a divine child; Mary to whom God had whispered his holy truth!

Truly she was an Artist, a prophet, a messiah!

An inexplicable joy welled up within her: she was moving towards the life she had always imagined was waiting for her. It seemed that everything unpleasant was far away, that the best part of her life was only beginning.

# CANTO EIGHT § LOVE IS A GRAND SUBTERFUGE

# 1

But my Cordelia: I imagine you shaking your head; you do not approve! I hear you even in this place: what is that you called me? Ah yes: a false prophet, dispensing false parables! You laugh at my Professor and Artist and Seeker: the blunt instruments with which I pursued my lofty ends!

But halt! you cry: it was only moments ago that you spoke of your Cordelia's praise! We are to accept that now her absolving voice mocks you with your failures? Yes: does such an alteration seem strange, improbable, absurd? I assure you that it is not, wish that such was the case! For soon my Cordelia's approval gave way to a vague and distracted ambivalence, punctuated by overt dismissal: our subsequent encounters were characterized by her reticence. How earnestly I yearned to again elicit her praise; how it pained me that I could not! Climbing the hill to my garret those nights she never arrived, or occupied the chair opposite in silence, I returned again and again to the memory of her onetime approval, forced to content myself with my heart's (lessened) response to memory (just as the bereaved must to dreams of their lost love, or lingering ghosts!). What sorrow that eventually no stock remained within memory's store, that recollection failed to inspire my heart from its indifference and malaise (ambivalence overtook concern; on some nights, far past drunk, I fancied that I no longer cared if I lived or died)…

But enough: this prelude is only to illustrate with what earnest feeling I sought to again capture some small *miettes* of that praise that once enlivened and upheld me! I produced page upon page; her indifference never wavered; how like a child I sat before her! (Yes, like a child before its mother: I bore her perfect love, hung on her every word and look and gesture as the direct and final and heavenly verdict of my worth!)

(How little I understood then! How the Absurd Man within me laughs!)

But I will be brief! I sat for weeks before her, began to sense a change: alongside my reverent adoration grew another feeling, grew something malicious: the Devil within me spurned her, criticized her, called her base (common, philistine!), saw no transcendent light but only an unimaginative town girl whom a poorer player would not fail to move; soon my spite overwhelmed my hope, and with secret malevolence I constructed one in whom I saw no redeeming qualities, one which my Artist's heart mocked, of which the slightest word of praise would reveal my Cordelia as laughably inexpert…

Yet of my blunt instruments she loved him best and I, like a lover spurned, forwent my previous spiteful distance and again supplicated myself to the necessity of her adulation: how I laugh to think of it now; Claudio my clown became my great hope! Silly Claudio who I invented with only spite in my heart, whose ignorant crisis was to me the proxy for the uneducated and unfeeling world! Yes; Claudio who met his mistress only because his luggage was lost along with hers, who offered to buy her dinner, who did not admit to himself what was happening until she was in his hotel room, undressing. How absurd that he has become my redemption! And how absurd his crisis: consider what follows!

> The telephone woke him: his wife had been so worried! And why hadn't he called when he arrived? Speaking softly (his mistress was still asleep beside him) he explained that his luggage had been lost, and he had simply forgotten in the confusion. Hanging up he felt a strange sensation; he could see neither floor nor opposite wall (he had not turned on the bedside light), and he imagined that the darkness before him was not the shadows of his hotel room but was rather Oblivion

swelling to swallow him, a pit which had miraculously opened at his feet and into which he was now falling... He was hypnotized by that seemingly vast emptiness beneath him...

(Yes: and in the morning he was wracked by guilt, could not eat, wished to fall from life: he had dreamt (with his new mistress asleep beside him) that he could not move, that his wife kissed his cheek and he could not turn to kiss her mouth, that he could not pet his children's heads, that (though he wished to cry out!) his mouth and tongue remained immobile, that he could not so much as raise his hand in a loving gesture when they all departed; does it still please you to know his laughable and simplistic despair, his philistine postulation? How I laughed when I wrote them! And his uncertain consideration (his wife would not be bettered by knowing; a single indiscretion, if never repeated, counted for nothing against their life together; such secrets could only engender an impossible distance; he could not bear it on his conscience); how I despised him, writing that he vacillated between these extremes, at turns certain that each was correct! (And that he still had not decided when his wife met him at the baggage carousel (his luggage had, eventually, been located and returned to him); that he decided to postpone the decision, but that of course on the next day he was busy at work (the results of his trip had to be promptly and efficiently filed and reported!); that he reasoned that it was impossible to make such an important decision under such conditions, again decided to wait; that he continued this delay until it was time again for him to travel to her city; that he called from the airport (she had left her telephone number on the bedside notepad, he had thoughtlessly placed it in his wallet, he was later surprised to find it) and invited her to dinner, that afterwards he fell asleep beside her, and I laughed and again condemned him to dreams of unprecipitated paralysis...)

## 2

Why had he done it? And why, too, hadn't the evening's obvious progress confronted him, inspired the appropriate sense of transgression and betrayal? Claudio took his greatest delight in those of his wife's experiences that did not include him: the idea of his wife as one whose experience and perspective differed wholly from his own filled him with adoration and a visceral yearning and he imagined her as an autonomous world, whose wonders a lifetime of exploration could never exhaust. When (after they had been married for some time) her stories became familiar and her new experiences mundane (at best) or shared (at worst) he became frustrated: perhaps she did not hold so vast a store of fascination as he had once assumed! Was it possible that he was mistaken, when he saw in her an autonomous world whose wonders a lifetime of exploration would never exhaust?

Despairing over the fascinating woman he was certain he had lost, he did not think about the past; likewise the thought of the coming years (years he would spend patiently listening to her pedestrian stories, resolving her petty concerns) burdened and oppressed him. As a result he thought neither of past nor future, but lived instead in a vague limbo of undefined waiting, for years concerning himself only with the day-to-day occurrences of their unremarkable lives.

Mired within this ever-present disappointment and resignation the appearance of another (who fascinated him, who seemed an autonomous world) wholly overwhelmed his thoughts, and he went to bed with her without hesitation. It was only in the morning (waking to find not his wife beside him, but another there instead) that it occurred to him what he had done.

# 3

But I have introduced him enough: here are those pages!

He made quarterly visits to her city, they fell into a familiar routine; interludes of concentrated proximity (he called her from the airport, she met him at his hotel; he left only for meetings) interspersed prolonged absences. Soon, hoping to both express his growing fondness and alleviate his undeniable anxiety (that during their separation some change would cause her to prohibit future rendezvous), he began to punctuate their encounters with the following promise: even if his duties changed and he was no longer required to travel to her city, he would nevertheless continue his visits!

By this he meant that he was willing to undertake a grand and difficult subterfuge (he would of course tell his wife he was traveling on business, a delicate and easily undone fabrication; without company backing he would be responsible for the expense), and assume as a burden that which had previously been characterized by convenience.

This willingness to be burdened for the sake of another comprised, to Claudio, an unambiguous declaration of love; the grand subterfuge implied an irresistible passion which he, in imagining it, was certain that he felt. Yes, there was no greater love than that which was willing to burden itself in the name of its beloved! Staring into her face, overcome with emotion (the powerful emotion his promise conveyed, the irresistible passion that necessitated grand subterfuge!), he felt certain that he was willing to undertake substantial burden and personal expense in the name of the love he bore her.

## 4

This declaration was, however, uniformly met with silence: did Claudio's mistress misunderstand him? No; she understood perfectly! By weighting himself with the burden of their affair he wished to compel - to burden - her as well. The promise never failed to amuse her: he was so childish, so earnest! He spoke his promise with all the conviction of one seeking absolution before the gallows.

The repetition of the promise and the intensity with which he spoke it, however, made it nearly impossible to dismiss: she found herself thinking of it at odd and inconvenient moments. This-or-that date was soon to arrive, this-or-that boyfriend said that he loved her; a vision of him promising that he would undertake the burden of their affair arose, unbidden, before her.

The irresistible longing (their meetings could not be halted; his heart demanded the grand subterfuge!), so often dismissed, eventually confronted her with its insistence; she began to envy Claudio the passion which would not be denied and which necessitated grand subterfuge. She had never felt such self-assurance! Even at her most impassioned moments her heart had remained mutable, subservient to reason. Yet perhaps love was the heart's mandate, against which one was powerless!

She tried to imagine herself submitted by an undeniable passion. She found that she could not: a thousand reasonable objections and resignations came almost instantly to mind. No, she could not love that way; what she felt for him justified only the meager effort presently required of her, justified only the meager effort she allowed herself. Were she asked to shoulder a substantial burden in the name of what they shared, she knew that she would put an end to their meetings.

The irony of this was not lost on her: in hoping to secure indefinite assurance of continuance, he had instead only helped her to define the limit of her affection for him. Perceiving her own limit, it seemed somehow inevitable that she would reach it; she began to long for the time in their relationship that preceded his declarations of irresistible passion. It was of no use: he continued to punctuate their meetings with promises of grand subterfuge. Painfully aware of her own limitation (that private and seemingly inevitable betrayal), she turned away and refused to speak.

(To what did Claudio attribute his mistress' reticence? A clown, knowing only his own expression, comes to believe in the sole authority of appearance; Claudio saw (in each new silence) a woman deeply moved, exchanging with him an unspoken understanding. Yes; she loved him, shared his burden; should his duties change and his trips become unnecessary, she would nonetheless devoutly wish his continued attention. Self-assured, he repeated his promise; she (again aware of the love she could not feel for him) turned away and remained silent.)

## 5

Bolstered by what he misunderstood to be her collusion Claudio became increasingly convinced that a life in which he was denied their quarterly meetings comprised an insufferable imprisonment within the staid confines of his own existence. It is worth noting, then, that prior to the advent of the promise his life had never seemed a prison; what does this signify? Did he come to realize that his life was a prison only after he came to regard it as such? Or did it appear a prison only because, voicing the promise to his mistress, he imagined high and carefully guarded walls over which he would be forced to climb? Voicing his willingness to undertake the burden of inexcusable travel and personal expense and receiving (what he took to be) a signal of her accord, he gave himself over to the emotion (growing affection and lingering anxiety) that had prompted his initial promise; in doing so his own familiar world became (in his view) the antithesis of happiness (which resided in another city with his mistress) and began to needle him with the threat of a prolonged and difficult (denied the excuse of his routine business trips the affair's continuance would come to require a grand subterfuge) internment.

Likewise he came to feel that the love he bore his mistress was a great and tragic love, a love cruelly denied by the world, for which he was willing to undergo significant hardship (anxiety and personal expense!): the passion he felt (passion which necessitated a grand subterfuge!) measured against the world's endless obstacles (their affair continued only by the grace of the world's indifference; their peace was a fragile one!) produced in him a sense of ardent immediacy; he felt a love unlike any he had known before (it was the antithesis of what he and his wife shared!) and concluded that at all previous declarations of love he had misspoken, that it was only towards his mistress that he had ever felt real love.

(Why not, then, leave his wife and children, relocate to her city and there pursue a life in greater proximity to the object of his delight? Why not follow his heart! He felt a compelling aversion toward this possibility; the reasons he provided (he would not abandon his children, he was working towards partner at the architectural firm) disguised and dismissed his concern that, were the world altered in such a way that their affair no longer constituted a grand subterfuge, he would grow quickly disenchanted, and would find that he had exchanged one prison for another.)

## 6

He called her from the airport and she met him at his hotel; afterward she stood in front of the bathroom mirror and considered herself from a number of angles. He watched her from his position on the bed; what was she doing? And was she coming back to bed? Without looking away or answering him she reached out and closed the bathroom door.

What was she doing? She was observing the evident revisions time had made upon her body. It occurred to her (as though a revelation, although she had not previously been unaware of the obvious fact) that she was getting progressively older, that times that had passed were now unrecoverable. Had she imagined that she could return to them? Certainly not! And yet the fact that she could not now seemed newly-present and unbearably painful.

Certain moments from her youth, deceased friends and relatives, that morning's coffee: all were lost forever! The memory of each mocked her with its infinite intangibility. How was it that she was denied the past? It seemed impossibly cruel.

(And to what end? For when she died her memories would come to nothing, would vanish along with her…)

Considering herself in this inevitable progress she was confronted and horrified; looking into the mirror she imagined that she saw herself as she would look laying in her casket, all of her memories forgotten. (She touched her cheek; yes, even her skin was cold!) But at that moment he called to her from the bed; was she hungry? He was going to call down for something to eat! She smiled: his voice, his presence, even his mundane hunger were, somehow, a profound relief.

What was this relief? Standing in the bathroom she was mired in recollection (which taunted her with pleasures she could not reclaim) and postulation (which horrified her with the apparition of her own end). But hunger is the visceral present; hunger is the antithesis of memory and forecast! Yes, she was hungry; inspired by a swell of affection she left the bathroom and embraced him…

## 7

Silly Claudio (knowing only his own expression) saw in her reticence a profound communiqué, yet discerned nothing noteworthy in her vigil before the mirror, her retreat into the bathroom; he did not think of it again and was therefore taken by surprise when, calling from the airport on his subsequent trip, she apologized and replied that she could not see him. He began to protest: what did she mean? And what was wrong? She only repeated that she could not see him; before he could reply, she hung up.

He was certain that, if he stood before her, she could not refuse him; he hailed a taxi and gave the name and address of her building (once he had picked her up outside). The driver let him out; did the doorman know which apartment was hers? He was a friend come in unexpectedly from out of town: he was hoping to surprise her! The doorman gave him the number; he rode the elevator up to her floor.

He knocked and called her name, the door opened; they moved through an unbroken series of gestures and responses and afterwards (they lay on her bed, he had covered himself with the sheet) he asked why she had refused to see him. She only shook her head; by this she meant to imply that the question and its prompting action were of no great consequence. Claudio (knowing only his own expression) imagined instead that her behavior denoted final refusal, and imagined that this second refusal was her punishment for his having dismissed the first. (Her silence, then, was an assault; overwhelmingly irritated (the familiar progress of their encounter had rapidly devolved into a maddening debacle, confronting him at every turn with some new refusal!) he went into the bathroom and closed the door…)

# 8

Why had she refused? Because it seemed there was nothing else to do; lying beside him on their previous encounter (the vision of herself as she would appear, presented in her coffin, had not yet fully dissipated; he was on the telephone, calling down to the kitchen) she felt an aching affection for him, a visceral necessity that composed the world into binary opposition (Claudio and all-that-was-not-Claudio) and saw in her own life (the life she lived during his prolonged absences) nothing of value and in their shared life (the vibrant life she lived during their brief proximity) the only worthwhile moments she had spent since the affair began.

(Was it true that the only worthwhile moments she had experienced in the previous three years had been those spent in his presence? Yes; in that moment (he was arguing with the steward about what time the kitchen closed) she was certain that all moments spent apart paled in comparison to those spent together. Imagining her own death she experienced a profound sense of her life's weightlessness (when she was dead her memories, her concerns would be wholly forgotten!); likewise the rational composition of their affair (his quarterly visits, the familiar phone call from the airport) seemed a ridiculous confinement through which her heart's true yearning had been unjustly funneled.)

How profoundly she loved him; how she yearned to love him openly, to be freed from the grand subterfuge!

Later, she recoiled from this feeling; how ridiculous she was! Certainly she knew better! After all: she was a realist! Did she imagine that he would leave his wife? Certainly not! The realities of their affair (and its limitations) had been clearly established from the outset. And yet now the careful order was thrown into disarray; she had fallen in love with him! (How absurd: that love should appear as a telephone call to the kitchen, as an argument with the hotel steward! But at that moment she had known: yes she had clearly known!)

There was nothing else to be done; she was no longer young, or as pretty as she had been; how long would it go on? Would she stay in love with him until she was too old for anyone else? Perceiving that her life (whose remainder, in her moment before the mirror, had seemed insignificant, brief, ever-fleeting and soon to be concluded) could be spent bound by love to a regimented sequence of meetings and absences, she replied that she could not meet him.

## 9

In the bathroom the shower came on; she was struck by the thought that he was trying to wash away any physical trace of their meeting. She had a sudden desire to join him; not to continue their lovemaking, but to wash him away as well.

And suddenly she laughed; yes, she laughed out loud! Many of her friends professed to showering after making love; many of her own lovers had showered after making love to her. (One, she remembered suddenly, had even insisted on brushing his teeth, fearing that his wife would taste her lips on his!) She had always enjoyed the lingering sensation of her lover's body upon hers; why would she wish to erase it? Now she understood! The lingering sensation of his body was too much for her to bear; yes, she would wash away any trace his body had left on hers, and would do so before his astonished eyes! (And not only him, but herself: her familiar body and the inevitable progress that made her love a prison (were it not for the presence of time her years spent loving him, waiting for him, would be insubstantial, forgotten!); her ridiculous heart that found such delight in this oblivious man…)

She crossed the room and tried the bathroom door; it was open; she was unsure of what to do! She thought of the first night they had met; how strangely she had acted! She really was not like that at all! But wasn't that the woman he was thinking of, when he called her on subsequent trips? Wasn't she the woman he returned, once every quarter, to see? She opened the door and went inside.

Afterwards they lay drying on the sheets as it grew dark. Eventually he fell asleep, and she slipped from beneath his arm. She went into the bathroom and stood looking at her own reflection.

She had the vague sense that this was a momentous event, a dramatic turning point in her life. But its exact implications eluded her: she was not certain what in her had changed nor what would, in the future, be altered. She stood considering it for some time. When she returned to bed she discovered that, in her absence, he had rolled onto his side and now lay facing her. She was surprised by how noticeably time had changed him. He looked so much older than he had three years earlier! So time was pursuing him as well! She was somehow comforted by this fact. She crawled into bed beside him.

Her heart was filled with love and the certainty that whatever difficulties lay ahead would inevitably be sorted out. Not without some effort, it was true! But the burden of this effort seemed a light one, and if not light then at least one (she was dreamily certain) that she would willingly shoulder for the sake of their love.

# CANTO NINE § MAN GOETH HIS LONG WAY HOME

# 1

What became of Claudio?

Eventually his responsibilities changed, and he was no longer required to make quarterly visits to the city where his mistress lived. He continued to see her for the year that followed, but grew increasingly anxious: what if his wife spoke with someone from his work, and learned that his travel was not business-related? What had been a pleasurable and convenient arrangement became increasingly burdensome: eventually he explained to his wife that his responsibilities had changed, that he was no longer required to travel. He did so without offering any explanation to his mistress; he had made certain that she did not have any numbers at which to reach him, and so was not surprised when he did not hear from her. In this way, the affair ended without announcement or fanfare.

With the affair ended, and with no future encounters to protect, he became needled by guilt; the affair had seemed to constitute, at the time, a separate world, a second life, which owed no explanation to the first. Yet with his travel indefinitely suspended he came to feel that this was not the case: that indeed the affair constituted a betrayal, a dalliance from his life, the only life he had. Eventually, regarding this guilt, he made a full confession to his wife, who cried and expressed her wish that he had not told her. Knowing did her no good; it only caused her pain! (This response surprised him; he had never imagined that she would rather not know.)

Following his confession he had felt the affair hanging about his neck, as though at any moment he might be hauled before the jury, and forced to explain.

## 2

His children grew up and moved away, and with them gone he found himself living in the vague limbo of his wife's indifference. She paid little attention to him, and regarded it as her own business what she did while he was at work. His habits and behavior seemed to disgust and annoy her; she seemed to resent his presence. She began to sleep in their daughter's unoccupied bed; he suspected that she would have been happier alone.

He had befriended a young woman at work; they worked on many of the same deals and often spent their lunch hour together. Eventually their conversations turned to personal matters; he suspected that his wife resented his presence, and would rather live alone! The others at work began to kid them: Romeo and Juliet of the office! They laughed together at this joke; how ridiculous, that anyone would think that about them! After all, he was almost old enough to be her father! But privately this suggestion excited him; was it possible? The prospect was too fantastic to dismiss; it had been so long since he had felt this way!

The young woman knew about his previous affair, and sympathized: his wife was being too hard on him! He was a man, and had a man's needs; if she was not satisfying them at home then it was her own fault that he was forced to go looking! And it was unfair for her to lord it over him all of these years; after all, she was not perfect herself! Besides: he had admitted that he was wrong; what more did she want from him? It made no sense for him to change if his efforts went unacknowledged!

One afternoon (the weather had turned unexpectedly warm) she invited him back to her apartment (she lived on the other side of a nearby park, it would be a pleasant walk) on their lunch break. After they finished eating he laughed: they had better get back, or people would talk! But she did not laugh; did they really have to go? She did not want to go. He responded that they did not have to go if she did not want to. But was she sure? He meant: he was old enough to be her father! She nodded, then took him by the hand. He presented no further arguments.

## 3

Afterwards he was again overcome with guilt; why had he done it? He did not know; he did not know! And should he tell his wife? And did it matter? And who would the young woman tell? And would they know, regardless? And why had he been so stupid? And why hadn't he insisted that they leave? And what now? He was unsure of what to do, and so he did nothing.

The only context in which he could understand this indiscretion was in terms of his previous one; he searched his memory for some cue as to how to act. But he soon abandoned his search: his last affair had been a hopeless failure in which he had done nothing right! It was ridiculous to search through it for guidance. Knowing that no good could come of it, he nonetheless confessed to his wife. He had been weak; he had been stupid! Could she find it in her heart to forgive him? He would do anything; he would do whatever it took to make it up to her!

Having so thoroughly considered his previous experience, he was surprised to find that his new confession did not inspire her tears. She nodded, as though agreeing to something she had not voiced. He knelt down before her; he was on his knees, begging her forgiveness! Could she find it in her heart? She did not know; she would have to think about it. She packed a bag and went to stay at a motel.

He returned home from work each day for the following week, hoping to find her car parked in the driveway. At the end of the week he found a moving truck parked on the street outside, and men carrying things out of the house. Where were they taking her things? They had an address for an apartment across town. He called the number listed on the form, but when she heard his voice she hung up.

## 4

Soon the affair was known at the office, and he was called in for a meeting with his superiors. He had been a valuable asset to the firm, and they appreciated his years of dedication and hard work! Nevertheless they felt that circumstances required that they be frank: his situation was a detriment to the culture of the business. Perhaps he was not aware; the young woman had been transferred into his department when a similar situation arose at her last position. Regardless, the partners felt that she had a promising career ahead of her; and he was already at an age where it was not unheard of for him to retire. Having worked with her, they were sure that he could see what a shame it would be to lose her! They were prepared to offer him a handsome retirement package; they had the paperwork right here!

Afterwards he did not feel like going out, and left his house rarely. When he did it was only to meet with lawyers who informed him of the difficult months and possibly years that lay ahead. He called the young woman; he needed to talk to someone! But she did not answer or return his calls.

He felt a void opening before him; the life he had known seemed suddenly strange and far away. The life he lived now had none of the familiar comforts; it lacked even the reassurance of familiar burdens!

How ridiculous this new life was; how absurd! It would be easier, after all, to leave it. They would be sorry, then; they would be sorry for all the ways they had wronged him! He left his car running in the garage and went upstairs to bed.

As he fell asleep he imagined that he heard someone singing; of course! It must be the angel choir in heaven. They called his name; they knew all things which shall be hereafter upon the earth! Listening to them, he knew that he had made the right decision. He closed his eyes and went to sleep.

## 5

The car ran out of fuel and the engine stopped; later the battery died, and the car turned off. For two days he lay undisturbed, and on the third day his wife called; she was coming over to pick up a few things. Would she call him back when he got the message so that they could arrange a time? A while later his lawyer called; could he give them a call back at the office? His wife called again; he could not just ignore her! She had some errands to run; she was going to stop over on her way home, and would appreciate it if he wasn't there. She arrived several hours later, and found him in their bed.

She called the police, who called the coroner; the body was removed and she went downstairs to call their children. But neither of them were at home; she left messages for them to call her as soon as they got in. The sheriff took her aside and offered the name of a funeral home; she called and made arrangements for them to pick up the body. Of course; if she left their number with the medical examiner the funeral home would be informed whenever the medical examiner was finished. She could come by at her convenience with whatever clothes she would like him in. Also, there was the coffin to consider.

She pressed a hand to her forehead; there was so much to do! And she still had to contact the lawyer; she had not yet spoken to her children. The funeral director reassured her; she needn't worry, they would take care of everything! She thanked them and hung up. An officer came over and, apologizing, explained that he did not want to bother her, but it was required that a report be filed for these sorts of things, and he needed to ask her a few questions.

It was all right; she did not mind. Had she been at home? No, she had come upstairs and found him. They were – she and her husband were – separated. They were going through a divorce. She had not spoken to him for several days. The policeman nodded;

all right, that was fine. He could see that she was in no shape to answer these questions now. Would she mind calling down to the station when she felt up to it? Not at all; he thanked her and left.

When they were gone she went upstairs; the sheet was stained and she took it off the bed. Then she tried her children again. There was still no answer; she left messages saying that she needed to speak with them as soon as possible. There was nothing else to do; she went out and got into her car. She sat in the driveway, crying. Then she dried her eyes and went home.

## 6

There was so much to do! Her son arrived with his wife and children and her daughter arrived with her husband and children. What could they do? How could they help?

Would her daughter help her pick out clothes for him to wear? And would her son sort through the cemetery brochures? There was a stack of them on the kitchen table. Certainly; whatever she needed! They left and she went into the kitchen to make dinner. Her daughter came in a while later; which of these jackets did she like better? And which of these ties? She was not sure; where was that nice one he used to wear at Christmas? Her daughter knew just which one she was talking about; she had not seen it, but she would look again.

Her son came in; he had found the perfect one! They could get side-by-side plots at this cemetery for a very good price, and they even offered a discount if they purchased the headstone from an associated mason. How did that sound? Whatever he thought best; would he take care of it? Certainly; he left the room. Her daughter came in bearing a suit before her; was this the one? Yes, it was perfect; she could leave it on the dining room table and she would take it herself to the funeral home. The notebook her husband had used for telephone numbers was upstairs on his desk; could her daughter call anyone she thought would want to know, and let them know the time and place of the funeral? She'd started to herself, but had run out of time.

The next morning they went to the church; the minister stood facing them as they sat in the first pew, and reviewed what would happen: they would open with a hymn, then he would say a few words. Then the family would have some time to speak. Afterwards the pallbearers would carry the coffin out, and he would direct everyone to follow them to the cemetery; there would be a limousine waiting outside to take them. From there it was very simple; he would read a passage and they would lower the coffin. He would scatter a handful of dirt on top, and they could each drop a handful of dirt into the grave as they went past if they felt so inclined, and then the limousine would take them to wherever they were having the reception. Did anyone have any questions? No; she thanked him and then led her children from the church.

Her daughter cried in the car; she could not believe he was gone! She just could not believe that a person could go just like that: just lay down to take a nap and be gone just like that! Her mother nodded; oh, yes, it was very strange! Imagined how she felt; she'd only gone out for a little while to run some errands, and come back to find him that way!

# 7

The pews were full; she walked to the front and thanked them for coming. What could one say at a time like this? Her marriage to her husband was almost all she knew. It had produced two wonderful children; it had given her a lot of joy; she regretted nothing of their time together! Now their daughter would like to speak; her daughter embraced her and then climbed up behind the podium. She could not believe her father was gone! There were just a few things she wanted to say; she unfolded her notes. Her father was; she was sorry! Her father; she pressed her hands to her face and sobbed. The minister took her arm; it was all right! He motioned to her brother, and the two of them led her down the steps.

The people shifted in the pews. His son got up to speak; there were so many things he had wanted to say – so many things he'd never had the opportunity to say – to his father. Maybe what was hardest was not that he was gone, but that now those things would never be said. He'd never told his father what really happened to the rear bumper of his car that time in high school; it had been years since he'd told his father that he loved him. And now his father was gone and what could he say, what could anyone say? He didn't know. He thanked them for coming. He took his white gloves from his pocket and put them on; the other pallbearers rose from their place behind the pulpit and one of them lowered the casket lid.

The minister invited everyone to follow them to the cemetery; the people in the pews rose as the coffin went by. Claudio's wife stood near the front and watched the coffin go down the steps to the waiting hearse. The minister asked if she was all right; she replied that she was fine. The people were shuffling out; a young woman looked at her and when their eyes met she looked away. The young woman turned and his wife watched her narrow waist and her good posture and her small, careful steps and the limp knot of blond hair that fell down her neck.

Someone said her name; she turned to face a woman older than herself. The older woman was sorry to bother her; she was not even sure that she should have come. His daughter had called and told her the time and place of the funeral. The woman seemed, suddenly, to change her mind; no, she should not have come! She turned and walked after the retreating crowd. But his wife called her name and she stopped and turned. She had wiped away the makeup where it ran down her face with her tears, but the creases around her eyes were deep with age and mascara still showed in the lines.

His wife went down the steps towards the woman and embraced her. She had wondered for so many years; she'd had no face for the person her husband had named. She'd wondered what she would do if they ever met. But now to meet her here, like this, both of them old and made the same by grief… It did not matter, now. She was glad that she had decided to come. Would she ride with the family to the cemetery? Yes; they walked together out of the church and into the waiting car.

# 8

They stood in a tight knot around the grave, the minister began to read; all go unto one place, all are of the dust, and all turn to dust again! They lowered the casket. His daughter wept against his son's shoulder. His mistress stood beside his wife; the young woman looked unwaveringly ahead. Then there was a strange sound and the minister went silent; one of the straps had snagged and the coffin had lurched and struck the side of the grave. The man operating the winch hurried around the front to look at the problem. After a pause the minister continued reading: Man goeth his long way home; then shall the dust returneth to the earth as it was, and the spirit shall return unto God who gave it!

The man reversed the winch and the coffin rose, slightly, then jerked to a stop. For he cometh in with vanity, and departeth in darkness, and his name shall be covered with darkness! The man operating the winch raised and then lowered the coffin, and the coffin stopped and bumped against the side of the grave.

His daughter sobbed; the minister stepped back from the grave. There was a murmur of conversation near the back, and a few of the men moved forward to examine the winch. His wife looked around; it was a beautiful, bright, clear day, and the cemetery was crowded with graves. They were standing in one of the only unoccupied places. It occurred to her, suddenly, that of course the unoccupied ground beneath her feet was her own grave: her son had purchased two side-by-side. She had an odd desire to tell the people to leave; they had no business standing on her grave! But she stayed silent and the feeling passed.

Suddenly there was a great noise from the winch; one of the gears rumbled and then the strap ran smooth and the coffin went down into the grave. There was a murmur of congratulations, and then everyone was silent again. The minister took a handful of dirt from the mound beside him and dropped it onto the casket. A line formed behind him, and everyone threw on a handful of dirt. Then there was no one left and they walked to the car. But his daughter stopped; the grave was still open, he was not all the way buried! They could not leave it like that! The minister assured her that the gravediggers would finish burying him. She did not move; her brother took her arm and led her to the car.

# 9

They went back to the house; the caterers were smoking outside the back door. When the cars began to arrive they crushed their cigarettes into the grass and went back inside. The family went up to the house: the grandchildren went first and fastest and then his children followed with their spouses and then his wife and his mistress. They filed inside and his wife went into the kitchen to put coffee on. But of course the caterers had already made coffee; one of them came in carrying teacups on a silver tray and then disappeared again. The funeral director had enlarged and framed a picture portrait of him and set it on an easel by the fireplace; his daughter had stopped crying in the limousine but started again when she saw it.

The mourners began to arrive; how was everyone holding up? It was such a shock; he had seemed in perfect health! Who knew why these things happened? They had to trust in God! Yes, God had called him home; he was at peace now with God! The food was delicious; had she tried any of the quiche? She really should try to eat something, even if she was not hungry. And how were his children taking it? And the grandchildren? Such a terrible thing; they shook their heads. If she needed anything, would she let them know? Anything at all! Their thoughts and prayers were with the family!

His wife went looking for his mistress and found her outside having a cigarette with the caterers. Did his mistress live in the area? No; she had booked a last minute flight. His wife nodded: the reception was mostly over; her children were going to take care of everything after the caterers were gone. She was thinking of going down the street for a drink; would his mistress join her? His mistress nodded; she crushed her cigarette into the grass and the two of them went inside together.

## 10

They were leaving; would her children take care of whatever happened while she was gone? She would be back in an hour or so. They went outside, but her car was blocked in by the mourners' cars. It was not far; did his mistress mind walking? Not at all.

They sat in a booth together and talked; two hours passed, and the conversation did not slacken its pace. Had he told her the story about this or that? And did she remember the face he made when he did not agree? And the way he looked in the morning, with his hair sticking up? He had looked just like a little boy! And the way that he looked at her; God it had been so long since he looked at her that way! Like she was the most precious thing in the world; like she was something rare and wonderful! Yes; she knew just that look.

Or the way he became angry sometimes; the way he said horrible things! And afterwards, the way he said that he did not mean them; of course they could not help but forgive him!

But how she had hated him sometimes! When he made their children cry or he lashed out or he buried himself in work and neglected them… No one knew it, but she had left him a month before he died; they had been in the process of divorcing; not even her children knew! She wept; he'd gone to his grave thinking that she did not love him! But it was not that; she did love him! It was only that there were so many years of hurt: by the end it had seemed impossible to fix, and easier to learn to live apart than to try to make it work living together. But he had died thinking that she hated him; she could not forgive herself for that!

But she had hated him; yes, she had! She had hated him and she had loved him and she had never figured it out. And now he was dead, and none of it would ever be worked out or resolved and so many things would never be put right! So many things: so many horrible things they'd done and said to each other!

# 11

This woman across from her was not so different from herself: they talked so easily and so enthusiastically that whatever transgressions one had waged against the other seemed long past and long forgotten. They drank and as the conversation went on his wife found herself wondering if there was a heaven, and that if there was, if one had this feeling always there: that all transgressions were forgotten, that the years of hurt no longer mattered. It seemed entirely possible: even probable, and seemed too that one day the three of them would sit there together: her husband, his mistress, and herself, and he would look at her, and she would again feel that she was something rare and wonderful, the most precious thing in the world. How she missed that feeling! They would talk and laugh together for all of eternity, and the joke would always be whether they remembered how important they'd once imagined they were, and how great their pain, and how, without resignation or bitterness, that it in the end it meant nothing, that it counted for nothing, that they were only a brief moment in an inconceivably vast ocean of time and space. How laughable it seemed; how great was God's grace!

She began to weep and, seeing her weep, his mistress began to weep as well. Why had she been so stupid? Why had she let it get so far? Why had she left? It was her fault; it was all her fault! She sobbed and the other patrons turned to look and then politely looked away.

## 12

They stayed for a long time, and eventually it seemed concluded that he had loved each of them in his own way, and that his love for one did not reduce his love for the other. His wife felt as though she had been a long time standing perilously on the brink of some terrible chasm, that at any moment the truth of her wasted life might confront her and in confronting, overwhelm her. But he had loved her (yes, he had loved her!), and this reaffirmation rendered moot this anxiety. She had dedicated her life to a man she loved, a man who loved her; certainly such was a worthwhile existence! His mistress was beautiful, fascinating, candid, alluring, but she could never have given him the life that his wife had! And if she'd done everything for love and that love was unrequited or trod upon then the love she felt in the performance of the act was reward enough.

They left the bar, and his wife marveled at his mistress; she seemed so self-possessed, so well composed! She felt tipsy and light and silly; she hadn't felt this way in years! She confessed that she did not drink very often; she had stopped when she became pregnant, and had rarely indulged since! But it was wonderful to feel this way; it was wonderful to feel as though nothing mattered very much and everyone in the world was your friend and that tomorrow would never come. She really should go home; her children would worry! And yet she did not want to go home; she was too wide awake. His mistress invited her back to her hotel room: they would have room service send up something to drink, and they could finish their conversation. They climbed into a cab; in the close space behind the glass his wife lay her head on his mistress' shoulder.

She had the strange sensation that they were best friends, had been best friends for a long time, and that something that had come between them had been resolved and they were free to again love each other without reservation. She closed her eyes and felt them moving: the road vibrating beneath the tires, the car swaying with the adjustments, the bone of his mistress' shoulder moving beneath her cheek, and each of these sensations filled her with pleasure that it was she and no one else here in this moment with each of these small and beautiful details to call her own.

They arrived at the hotel and went upstairs, and his mistress called downstairs for a bottle to be sent up. His wife was so happy: so very happy! She covered her face and wept into her hands. His mistress embraced her; his wife lifted her face to be kissed. As his mistress lowered her onto the bed there was a knock on the door; the bottle had arrived. The bellboy came in, carrying it on a tray with a bucket of ice and two glasses. He looked from one woman to the other without changing his expression. His wife sat up on the bed and unconsciously pulled the collar of her shirt more tightly closed. When he was gone they faced each other and for a long time said nothing; his wife covered her face. She should go; should she go? She stood and smoothed the front of her shirt. His mistress undressed, and stood naked before his wife. His wife wept; how could she ever thank her? They moved together onto the bed.

## 13

Afterwards his mistress opened the bottle and they laughed and it was only as the edge of the sky went gray and then yellow that his wife thought of her children. She went into the bathroom and showered and as she stood toweling off she caught sight of her reflection in the mirror.

For many years she had been noticing changes in her body; the skin along her neck had grown looser, her breasts began to sag, her hips spread, her stomach grew soft. Each of these changes seemed an isolated alteration to the body she'd had at twenty-five, the body she'd thought of as herself. Standing before the mirror, she saw that this was not the case: that each change was part of a trend that she had somehow refused to see or acknowledge. It was, rather, as though her body had been slowly replaced by another, and it was only once the transformation was complete that she noticed. She stood marveling: how fantastic it seemed that this mix of aches and features and familiar hues and sensations was herself!

She dressed, and as she did so she made up her mind: she was going to sell the house and move away. She imagined a life in a small apartment in a far away city. (She imagined a key turning in the lock; her husband's mistress came through the door. Her heart filled with happiness; their kiss was familiar yet exciting: it was the practiced kiss of those who have long shared each others' lives. City lights showed yellow against the black sky through the window; what a beautiful life! She had an impossible feeling of belonging, of embrace; yes, this was the life she had been waiting for!) She left the bathroom.

She supposed she had better be getting home; her children would worry! Perhaps they could exchange telephone numbers? She'd had a wonderful time; perhaps they could do it again? She did not mean; she blushed, laughed, and covered her face. But his mistress nodded; certainly. She wrote her number on a piece of hotel stationery and handed it to his wife. Give a call if she was ever in her neck of the woods! His wife nodded; she would! Well, she had to be going; she went to the door and went out.

# 14

She rode the elevator down in a giddy and trembling euphoria, clutching the piece of paper in her fist. But as she stepped out onto the street she felt a rising wave of exhaustion: the night without sleep, the days with her children, the funeral arrangements, the menu from the caterer, the parade of sympathetic faces, all confronted and overwhelmed her. She hailed a cab and slumped into the back seat; she closed her eyes and felt the cab begin to move, and was surprised to find that the sensation, which the night before had seemed so wonderful, now caused her to feel nothing at all.

The taxi stopped in front of her house; she paid and got out. The house looked dark against the pale pink sky; everyone was still asleep, and there were no lights on in any of the windows. She remembered that her husband was dead and that she had watched them lower him into the ground while she stood upon the spot where, in no more than a handful of years, she herself would be buried. She knew that she would not sell the house and very likely she would never see his mistress again, and that she would fade into old age as so many others had done: first gradually and then quickly, and then ultimately racing down that final black tunnel of years.

A light went on upstairs; her granddaughter was awake. His wife went inside; she could hear her granddaughter moving around on the ceiling above, then voices as her children came awake. She knew that soon they would come downstairs, and that soon afterwards there would be long talks: would she sell the house, and move closer to her daughter? Would she move closer to her son? They did not feel right, leaving her here all alone! There were nice apartments she could rent near them, where she would be around a lot of people her own age! Would she at least think about it? They just wanted to know that she was all right; they just wanted to know that she was safe!

And did he have life insurance? And what would they do with his things? And could she file their taxes? Did she have an accountant? And what would they write on his headstone? And did they have much savings? And who would pay what bills? And would she have a full physical done? At her age she needed to pay close attention to her health!

These were things she needed to think about!

## 15

She was so tired; she wished they would go away, and leave her in peace! Was it so much to ask, to be allowed to sleep in one's own house? She did not care about life insurance or apartments or accountants; she did not care about taxes or physicals or epitaphs! He was dead; what else could matter?

It seemed a fantastic joke; there was life and there was death, and death made life very simple. Life was just a series of directions and misdirections leading from nothingness to nothingness; the mother fed of the animals which fed of the earth and the child grew inside of her and was born and then aged and gradually returned unto the earth from whence it came. And in between came a lot of nonsense about taxes and mortgages and test scores and someone looking at her as though she was something rare and wonderful. Then all of that ended and what good did it do? What good had it ever done?

Her granddaughter came downstairs; had she slept well? She was growing up so fast! Would she like some breakfast? She could have anything she liked! No she was not sad; she was crying because she was happy to have everyone here together; it was nice to have everyone here together, wasn't it? Her granddaughter could go into the kitchen and pick out the cereal she wanted; Grandma would be right in!

She went into the bathroom and, once the door was closed, collapsed into sobs. But this outburst did not last long; she was too tired to maintain either the thought or the emotion that had inspired it. She dried her eyes and left the bathroom. Coming through the living room she heard crying from the kitchen: her granddaughter had overturned her cereal bowl as she was pouring the milk; milk and cereal formed a broadening puddle beneath the table. His wife knelt down beside her granddaughter; it was all right! Nothing to worry about; it was just a little spill! Grandma would have it cleaned up in two minutes.

But this did not help; her granddaughter continued to cry. His wife embraced her: she did not need to cry; everything was going to be all right! She would just get a towel and clean up the mess. Then there was the furniture to rearrange; the caterers had set the food out on the dining room table, and placed the chairs in an adjoining room. Then she really should decide what to put on the headstone. It did not make sense to buy two when it was perfectly acceptable for them to share one as man and wife: and after all, headstones were expensive! She would decide what she wanted written that afternoon. That way, when the time came, there would be one less thing. Everything seemed very clear, and she knew that she would have little trouble completing these final tasks.

# CANTO TEN § THE SIRENS

## 1

Have you concluded, then, that Claudio's mistress and the singing girl are one and the same? Did you reason (as I hoped you would!) that the lover who brushed his teeth was Costard himself? Certainly you have, certainly you did; I applaud you! (And discovered, too, that Costard's wife was Hermione's sister: how clever I imagined myself at the time of their writing; how godlike in my skillful orchestration! How the Devil within me laughs!)

(And so (you say) I have invented a laughable hyperbole, a parody: a girl who delights only in the pursuit of married men, to whom romance is inextricable from the ever-present threat of ruin: an artless Siren, guilelessly composed!)

Yes, she is (they all are) ridiculous, laughable: yes, I laugh at these pages! And doubtless you as well: seeing now my *ensemble* in commingled totality do you too dismiss them, find them improbable, unlikely, ridiculous? Having arrived at their union do you gaze backwards and cast your final verdict, charge that it was neither Homer nor Camus that inspired these pages, that their inglorious origin lies with none but their author's neuroses, his naïve desire to be understood, proclaimed clever, acknowledged and absolved? Certainly you do; certainly you are correct! (Yes, I submit and confess: these pages illustrate no profound revelation, reveal only their author's madman yearning and anxiety, his desire to stand in earnest before an absolving God, an anointing Angel, blessed *providence*…)

## 2

Yes: these actors own no other origins but my own bedeviled and multifarious self, exist only to enact my neuroses, passions, fantasies, perversions (whatever depraved arose from them arose from me); I proffer no further refutation, will offer no more fables of Algerian streets, of soiled bedclothes, of felled blackbirds; I will claim no external nor profound impetus! (Nor will I cite ethereal need and misplaced energies, the brandied praise of my elders, the intoxication of first fame! No transcendent hope abides, nor pilgrim's heart endures; these sordid pages reflect a sordid nature which no revision may erase nor ink stain soften! O, my thoughts be bestial, banal, worldly, fallen!)

Yes: precious little remains; that voice of pride that once imagined in my curséd brain some transcendent sight is silenced! (And what fire I feel now roaring in me! For my pride thus vanquished I might clothe myself in the most profane, might enact with impunity all that from which I fled: I might revel in all unholy and philistine endeavors and seek only corporeal – only animal, hedonistic! – delights! How wildly my heart thunders!)

Yes: I will no more endeavor to hide myself from myself, to color with prose the shameful revealed; how ridiculous I was to attempt such obfuscation! (Like one who, having dreamt a too-articulate dream, seeks instead to decipher its import with sophistry, seeks to ignore the translation his heart readily offers…) And so I now turn my gaze like an arrow shot towards the sun, falling back to strike he who let fly! What of these shameful indiscretions, this sordid history, this litany? What does it signify that I have contrived such action, that I compelled my Costard and blighted my Artist, that I harbored in my Claudio's wife an unprecipitated longing? Some explanation is owed!

(But first – forgive the interruption! – I must offer the following: all charges must be presented before the trial may precede, before the sentence may be rendered; so too I will offer up all transgressions and shameful offerings, will hide no damning mark!)

They were going out; Costard and Leontes could look after the children! They went down the steps, Hermione took her sister's arm; wasn't it wonderful to be together again? She could hardly express her happiness! (Her former melancholy seemed somehow impossible; it was as though she had been having a terrible dream whose horrors seemed ridiculous upon waking!) They'd had such a wonderful trip, had met such wonderful people, had seen and done such wonderful things: it was all too much! Her Artist's heart (she folded her hands upon her breast) long asleep was now again awakened!

They went into a café and took a table near the back. Costard's wife excused herself and went into the bathroom. With the door locked she removed her clothes, and with her clothes removed she felt a sudden pulse of excitement; what if she had forgotten to lock the door? What if someone happened to come in? And what if someone was crouched outside, peering through the keyhole? She allowed the sensation to linger for a moment before checking the handle.

She felt as though she had been walking for a long time, with both path and destination clearly in mind. Now, chancing to look down, she saw that she was not moving forward but was, in fact, enacting a progressless and solitary march over an endless void, whose depths now threatened to swallow her.

What was this void? She imagined a chasm, a pit bound in by cliffs. How ridiculous her life seemed, built, as it was, on nothing more substantial than her ignorance! Costard's moods, Sunday laundry, Monday shopping, the weekly rotation of dinners, the familiar quiet in the hour before bed, the brief litany of conversations, the alternate mornings driving their son to school, her customary and constant concerns, were all part and parcel of a world that seemed suddenly alien. The familiar structure of her week confronted and overwhelmed her; how arbitrary it all seemed! She had spent years constructing it, and yet now it seemed that her life held nothing for her; it was a comfortably appointed room whose windows looked out onto brick and mortar walls and whose doors opened onto barren deserts and wasted fields…

She dressed and returned to the table; her sister smiled warmly. They talked for some time about the things her sister had seen. Later the conversation changed, became instead about what color the walls should be in the entryway. Hermione insisted that they looked fine; her sister was unhappy with them and had already made up her mind to change them. They considered several options. But each color presented problems: if she picked this color she would have to change the whole interior; if she picked that color then the upholstery would have to be redone. They continued talking after the dishes were cleared away, and the conversation drifted away from and returned to the color to paint the entryway.

Leaving the table (the conversation seemed concluded) Costard's wife could not forgo her preoccupation. Everything else was the way she wanted it; if she could only fix this one last thing! It was her home, and she had the right to have it look the way she wanted! Yet it seemed that she would never discover the perfect shade: was it the color of this or that? And where had she seen it before? She did not know; she could almost see it; it was so frustrating! She knew that if she happened upon the color she would recognize it immediately...

# 3

And now I hear you protest, saying "Some explanation is owed for these poor sublimations, these ridiculous disguises!" (For art is more translation than alchemy, and these assembled and absurd *tableau* carry little significance beyond that instilled by my own insane explication! Yes: your failure in understanding is my failure in explanation!)

(It matters little, explanation is inevitable: such disguises dissipate in the face of circumstance! These stone walls offer no distraction, no haven of pleasant thought: here I am myself surrounded only by myself, unable to flee from myself; there can be no retreat, no sublimation, no hiding oneself from oneself…)

I have stated that I did not share my peers' egalitarian cravings, that I did not thrill to every passing girl, and sense in her an alluring possibility, but found rather there the horror that I might be seduced, overpowered by yearning (as I had heard it whispered sometimes occurred!) and forever stained by whatever indiscrete moments we shared. (What was the nature of the stain I feared? And what corruption did I imagine such indiscretion might engender? Certainly not least among these vague nightmares was the fear that such would make me somehow like that huddled and philistine horde, would erase those cursed distinctions that I had (though I called them curse!) come to cherish as mine and mine alone…)

And yet this awakened anxiety is hardly the beginning, nor the whole of it! For in the preceding years (while my classmates, attuned to their age, played at footraces and catch-the-crook) I was drawn – forgive the well-worn expression! - as moth to flame by the Kouros, by Botticelli's *Three Graces*, by those assembled and various portrait nudes I discovered housed in the pages of weighty tomes in my father's study; how many clandestine hours I passed tracing (and re-tracing!) curved lines of (soon familiar) images; how lovingly my eyes caressed those erotic and yet holy – those worldly and yet transcendent - figures!

(And how viscerally I recall my fluttering heart, my straining ears! For it seemed at every moment that I would be discovered by this-or-that passing maid, might be spied by some errant gardener wending his way along the shrubs outside the study window…)

And when no discovery came, how soon I grew bolder! For chance again conspired, our cook's niece paid a visit; how clearly I see her still! (It is a memory I have not revisited in a dozen years or more and yet here she again arises before me, with no detail lost: a face awash in dark curls, a slender hand reaching to clasp my own in greeting; a mere half-dozen years stood between us and yet I marveled at the transformation so little time could enact! And I, overcome with a potent trepidation that trembled my hand, rendered me mute…)

Yes: my hand trembled, but my mind was clear, certain, sure! For the cook's quarters were beneath my own: retiring to bathe following their lengthy drive our visitor left us; suddenly enlivened I (as children sometimes do) declared my irrepressible hunger: if I was not given some meager repast I would surely perish! Protesting the cook's departure (her niece's suitcase in hand, she had made to show the way) I clutched her apron strings and, through various cajoling laments, soon secured my prize: the cook, indicating the way to her niece, gave over the suitcase and instead absconded (from my clinging and crying!) to the kitchen; I, following close behind, made as though some inspiration had only just struck me: yes, I knew just what I desired, the only thing to satisfy my particular hunger! The cook rolled her eyes: certainly I could be satisfied with something simpler; that which I required would take substantial effort! I (sensing how near my final prize had come) gave myself over once again to earnest entreaties; my victim acquiesced; hardly able to disguise my agitation I retired to my room where, with my ear pressed to the grate, I listened hard (and with mounting tension!) for the sound of water in the basin…

## 4

And then: but I have not traveled through the corridors of this memory in many years! You will forgive me if I am reticent to face it (how strange that painful moments of youth should continue to so haunt and bedevil us, when childhood years are past)! That longed-for sound came, I left my room: carefully traversing the staircase (how each board protesting my meager weight wailed in my ears, became amplified by my fear!) I spied the cook through the kitchen door's small window (busily attentive to that superfluous task to which I had assigned her; my heart rejoiced in superior laughter, silently mocked one who could be so fooled by so small a boy!); leaving the staircase I entered the hall…

How the thought of that hallway still excites me! For the hall led only to the cook's quarters, and I had no previous occasion to enter there (even in those moments of childhood curiosity which drive one to explore all corners of one's minor world I, fearing discovery by that rotund and dominating figure, had regarded the hallway with aversion, had granted it wide berth); you can imagine, then, how my excitement was complimented by this transgression! I traversed the cook's quarters, beyond lay the sought-after door; the still-streaming water disguised my too-obvious footfalls; surreptitiously I pressed my eye to the keyhole…

Shall I describe what I saw? I am certain that you can imagine near enough! The bath stood opposite the door and she, standing to enter, cut so near a Botticellian figure that for a moment I lost all sense of myself, was again alone with my thoughts and wonder…

Would that I could have lingered there forever! Certainly I could not: the cook (I later heard her explain, had returned to inquire of her niece whether she, certainly hungry after her journey, would care for some of the same) discovered me kneeling at the door; ducking her admonishments (my heart thundering in my ears!) I fled; exiting the hall I turned up the staircase but lost my footing and fell; coming to rest on the landing (my body a cacophony of heretofore unexperienced pain!) I was met again by the cook, who hoisted me by my bruised arm (though I wailed!) and dragged me to the kitchen where, under her unwavering gaze I passed those hours that remained before my parents' return…

You cannot imagine my shame! For with every look and word the cook accused me; I sat before her as one awaiting the gallows. And yet it was hardly this that confronted me! For soon (seated before her) I discovered that I could neither articulate nor fully recall the reverent and pious nature of my spying; my genuflection seemed lost behind the gaze within which she fixed me and my act wholly stained by that ignominy which the cook, in her every gesture, implied.

Can you comprehend that horror? For, looking out into the world, I perceived no sympathetic ear: divested of its impetus and feeling the act became only the base transgression of the cook's accusing; horror, for my soul yearned to protest my innocence! My inarticulate tongue lacked the language to unpack with words my heart; horror, to find oneself muted behind the paper-thin (paper-thin and yet impassable!) veil separating one from another! What horror, moreso, for a young boy, bruised by his fall, awaiting the gallows…

(Perhaps you have experienced something of the same! I doubt that it is uncommon: what is the world to a child but an alien and unintelligible place, a hostile plane upon which their earnest (if inarticulate) protestations go unregarded, within which they find themselves hopelessly mute? How strange that such experiences do not linger, that men so readily forget how absurd the world remains!)

I prayed with all my soul that the cook would spare her niece knowledge of the episode, my prayers were in vain: I sensed in the girl an unmistakable change (she would not meet my eyes, held my hand only lightly as the evening grace was given), such as to make ridiculous any hope that she did not know…

## 5

Ah, but childhood is the time for such initial, laughable missteps! Soon the girl left, the cook's attentions turned elsewhere, my parents' awkward regard dissipated, the episode was forgotten… Yes, forgotten by all but myself! That horror (that I might be accused and ignored in my defense, that the world held no sympathetic ear) refused dissolution: likewise the sight of those ancient sculptures, those lovingly rendered nudes now filled me with self-loathing. (For my transgression, yes: but not for that alone! My loathing was also for that child who could mount no defense, whose impotent tongue and mind could enact no response!)

The volumes gathered dust, were soon moved, then moved again and the place forgotten, and soon enough lost to me; but not altogether! For certainly you are right to perceive something of that reverent regard in my later daydreams: what was my fantasy of the lost notebook, after all, if not that I might find one in whom something of that same transcendence lingered, to whom I might feel (might allow myself to feel!) unmitigated adoration? Such similarity is not so easily dismissed! (And now again the Devil within me laughs at my neuroses so obviously displayed! Yet I persist and protest: who but a statue can one love purely, unreservedly? I suspect that there is none, fear that unreserved adulation is a fantasy and nothing more…)

(But what, I hear you protest, of your Cordelia? Have you not only just finished telling of her praise, of your having achieved that ethereal regard for which you traversed the globe? How I laugh now at your ignorance! Yet again I can hardly fault you for your failure to know that which I have not revealed: you will know soon enough!)

# CANTO ELEVEN § "DEATH WOULD PUT AN END TO THESE MEAGER ORGANIC FUNCTIONS…"

# 1

Yes: I see now how much better it would have been had I cast these pages from me, burned them, scattered them across the river's waters so that they might lie beneath... How unwavering and unflinching is their mockery! It is with horror only that I see them here gathered before me; no dust of that trembling euphoria – that Artist's pride! – remains!

(Do I dare hope that my poor *ensemble* has touched you? Do I allow myself that blessed dream (that you might - as my Cordelia once did! - praise my efforts, might find amongst these scattered *tableau* something redeeming, some little remaining significance...)? No: such is too great a hope for such poor offerings! How I weep (how the Devil within me laughs!), these few lines comprise the falling gavel: that my aspirations have come to nothing, and I have failed!

Indeed: these pages hold no elixir, comprise no revelation, offer no salve, hold no absolution; I am as I was before that cursed day, when their composition inspired in me the fool's hope that I might transcend my bedeviled misery! Worthless, wretched I was; worthless, wretched I remain!

(Or do I dare hope that you find yourself wondering what became of my *ensemble*? Do you wonder where Costard was, while his wife stood in the café bathroom? I humbly (you cannot know how humbly!) thank you, bow to you, supplicate myself to your lightest word...)

Failing to overhear his wife's shouted declaration Costard left shortly after them: he drove to the girl's apartment but, receiving no answer to his knock, he went instead to the campus where he was informed by the secretary that the head of the department wanted to see him. He went down the hall, the department head called him inside: he would get right to the point! He understood that, during the spring semester, Costard had participated in a student anti-war protest in the course of which a fire was lit on campus, and local authorities summoned. Was this true? If it was true then the implications were very troubling, for – as Costard knew! - the college was facing significant pressure from the community to stifle any anti-war activity; he was certain he did not have to explain! Progressive thinking was a point of pride, but the policy regarding faculty was very different from that regarding students!

He paused; Costard, having no response, remained silent; the head of the department continued: he was sorry to bear the news! In light of the allegation, the administrators had decided that, pending a hearing with the college board, Costard should be placed on sabbatical until such time as that hearing could be held and a final verdict rendered. They would contact him when the date was set for that review; if he wished to submit an appeal he could do so at the President's office.

The head of the department was sorry; he knew it must come as quite a blow! He straightened the papers on his desk.

Did Costard have any questions? Costard blinked several times, then shook his head. Well then: if there was nothing else then he hoped Costard would excuse him; he had a lunch meeting, and had a great deal of work to finish up beforehand! Costard shook the hand extended to him. Also, they would need his office for whomever they hired to teach his classes; could he have his things cleared out by the end of the month? Costard knew as well as anyone how short they were on space! Costard nodded.

He went down to the parking lot, but could not remember where he had parked. Eventually he found his car, and drove to the girl's apartment. But again there was no answer to his knock; he went to look for her at the bookstore. Driving, he imagined that she might be standing at the upstairs window, singing behind the glass. But when he arrived the second floor window was empty; he went inside and saw her standing near the back, putting books onto a shelf. The thought of speaking to her, of answering her questions, of arranging a meeting, of offering excuses, wholly exhausted him. Before she could see him, he turned around and left.

He couldn't think of anywhere else to go; he drove home. Sitting in the car outside his house it seemed that there was no compelling reason to tell his wife what had happened. He decided, at least, to wait until after her sister was gone…

## 2

But now – please forgive the interruption! - I must interject a brief interlude, else surrender Costard's progress its (meager) logic (for which steps does one omit when illustrating one's own progress? Certainly intersecting fictions are no less necessary to one another!): you will recall that among the initial litany of Costard's distractions and disruptions I placed his wife's concern that their son had been leaving the house at night; where did he go? It is only too predictable! (But here: here are those pages…)

He paused beneath their place above the reservoir, she stepped from the shadow of the trees; he hurried to her; she took his hand and led him to the place where the blanket was spread beneath the lowest boughs. Afterwards she rose and descended the hill, and he watched as she dove and swam and then watched as she climbed onto the rocks on the reservoir's far shore. He wished that he had followed her, it was too late; she was already climbing the hill. He lay back, awaiting her arrival.

Did she know that he loved her, that she was his whole world? She was the only good thing in his life! She kissed him and got dressed. Would he meet her again tomorrow night? Yes; tomorrow night and every night! She kissed him and then continued on, up through the trees…

Above the city lights he could clearly see the stars, and was astounded by their number. He began to shiver, and felt a profound sadness; how sorrowful it was to be cold and naked and alone, staring out at innumerable and distant stars! His life, when considered against eternity, came to little: its span and whatever memory that remained after appeared and disappeared within a brief and forgotten interval. School, home, his mother's voice, familiar rooms, the cycle of days, recurrent tasks: his life seemed an arbitrary ritual performed at the altar of a cold and silent universe.

(He wished, suddenly, that he had followed her into the reservoir, that he had swum out to meet her and been overcome by a cramp, and drowned; he imagined them pulling his lifeless body from the water; it meant nothing! His funeral seemed a laughable and meaningless pageant; beneath the ground the years would pass like hours and it would not be long before the indifferent rain had washed the writing from his headstone…)

He stood and dressed. There were no lights on when he reached the house, and he went in through the back door and went downstairs to his room. He could smell her on his clothes, and wondered if he too had a smell, and if she could smell him and was thinking of him, too. It seemed ridiculous that, less than an hour earlier, he had thought of diving into the reservoir and sinking beneath its surface. The thought now filled him with desperate sorrow: he did not want to die! It seemed impossibly cruel that he should ever be taken from life…

## 3

He woke late and went out on the front porch; his aunt was sketching in a notebook. She was glad that he was up; she was getting lonely out here by herself! Would he come and sit with her? They'd had so few chances to get to know each other; his mother was always hovering around somewhere! But now he was practically all grown up, and she hardly knew him at all! She wanted them to be friends; could they be friends? She held up the sketchpad; what did he think? She was not entirely satisfied with it. Would he let her draw him? They could talk while she sketched his portrait.

How was he doing? And what did he like? And how was school? And was he making lots of friends? And did he like his classes? And did he have a girlfriend? And what did he think about things? Did anyone – his parents or his teachers – ever ask him what he thought? For example: what did he think of the war? In only a few years he and his friends would be eligible for military service; would he go and kill for his country? Would he go and die? (She could say for herself that she was opposed to the war; she was opposed to all war!)

She had met such interesting people on her trip, seen the most beautiful places! The world had again seemed vibrant with possibility; he did not understand, but one day he would! She had spent years trying to convince herself that the life she knew was all there was; she'd constructed innumerable excuses and retreats and dodges, with which she masked her cowardice! She'd been afraid: yes, afraid to expose herself to life; she could not tell him the thousands of ways she had learned to defeat herself! But the feeling on the road (dizzy and sleepless, too excited to close her eyes, afraid that she might miss something!) was a feeling she had almost forgotten that she knew!

She envied him; he had his whole life ahead of him! But would he turn a little this way? Would he part his lips just so? There: just a final touch! She turned the sketch so that he could see. What did he think? She tore it from the pad; he could give it to his girlfriend! He blushed. His mother called that lunch was ready…

## 4

…There was a knock at the door, his father came in; could his father speak with him? He knew this was a difficult time in his son's life; these in-between years were very difficult! What he meant was that it was not uncommon for boys to test the limits; it was perfectly natural! But at his age there were things that he was not ready for: things from which they (his parents!) had sheltered him. The world in which he was growing up in was a very different place from the world his parents had grown up in!

The thing he wanted to emphasize was consequences; one's actions always carried consequences! Responsibility: the most important thing was responsibility! They knew that he had been sneaking out at night; it was pointless to argue! They did not want him going out anymore! The Professor's son colored, then grew angry; it was none of their business! And why couldn't they leave him alone? He only wanted to live his life! He didn't tell them what to do; it was not fair!

Costard shook his head; he could be as angry as he wanted! It did nothing to change the fact: he was not allowed to leave the house after nightfall. Those were the rules! When he was old enough to move out he could do as he pleased; for now he expected his son to do as he was told! After all: his son was only a child, and knew nothing about the world! It was for his own safety; the world was a dangerous place! No responsible parent allowed their child to roam the streets at night!

There was nothing else to say; one day his son would understand! The Professor left the room, his son wept frustrated tears; there was nothing he could do or say! He felt oddly certain that, if he opened his mouth to speak, he would find himself rendered mute. His own weakness overwhelmed and exhausted him, and he pressed his face into the mattress and fell asleep. He dreamed that he was awake in his room, hovering six inches above the floor. Unable to touch anything, he was likewise unable to alter his position within the room. He called out for aid, but received no response.

He awoke several hours later and, climbing to the top of the stairs, saw in the window opposite that it was already dark. He heard his aunt and uncle talking in the next room. He sat down on the steps and waited for them to go to bed. Eventually he grew tired. He went back to his room and fell asleep.

## 5

And what was Costard doing, while his son sat waiting on the stairs?

...Costard stood at his bedroom window, watching the kitchen door below. He could hear his wife breathing in her sleep. After a while he turned to watch her and was confronted: she looked so vulnerable in her sleep! He was suddenly overwhelmed by his transgression. What had he done? And why had he done it? He had forsaken his life in a madness whose moment had come and gone but which, having transpired, did not cease but instead left open the door to further indiscretions. The full weight of his guilt pressed down upon him; how he yearned to confess (yes: confess and be absolved)!

The smell of the girl's skin, her questions, the books she read, the brief litany of their conversations, his tired excuses, the fear of discovery: the now familiar aspects of their affair confronted and oppressed him. He went to the bed and touched her shoulder; was she awake? He needed to tell her something! She murmured in her sleep; she rolled onto her back but did not open her eyes. Her cheek was creased by the pillow; the lines wove into those lines already forming around and beneath her eyes, stretching upward from her lips, running across her brow… He was startled; she looked so much older here before him than she had in his imagination a moment before! The prospect of watching her grow old, of sharing and enduring the coming years of inevitable and irreversible decline, repulsed him.

She reached up and touched his face; what was it? He cleared his throat: he had something to tell her! He had talked to their son like she had asked; their son would not be sneaking out anymore! She smiled; she lifted her face towards his and he bent, obediently, to kiss her...

…He went back to the window. A radio went on downstairs, and he heard her sister laugh. He felt an impossible longing. For what? He did not know. He thought of the girl; the sight of her singing behind glass was like a salve to his weary spirit! But this image was quickly replaced by thoughts of the girl herself, and he remembered, suddenly, that due to a prior engagement he would have to change the time of their next meeting. But of course that also meant that he would have to find some pretense to leave; further, he would have to remember to telephone from outside of the house (he certainly could not call her from here, with so many people who might hear and suspect!). Thinking of it exhausted him. He got into bed and was soon asleep.

## 6

And so: did his son's dalliances cease? You may discover for yourself!

...He went out the back door and up the hill; he said her name several times but received no reply. He sat down on the grass and wept; he'd never felt so alone! He felt somehow certain that the previous evening, when he had failed to meet her, she had slipped away from him and was now gone forever. How long had she waited for him? And with what mounting disappointment, frustration, hatred? He certainly could not blame her, if she assumed that his absence had been of his own choosing. How hurt she must be; how much she must hate him! (And how he hated his father, hated himself for the weakness that would not defy him!)

He heard a sound; was it her? He stood and called her name. Was she there? Had she come? He had not intended to break his promise; he was sorry! He stood and scanned the hillside and the lit areas along the road. Was she there? He was sorry!

No reply came: he gathered the blanket and descended the hill. He removed his aunt's portrait from his pocket and held it over the water (he would release it: yes, release it and watch the portrait sink, a fitting finale to their affair!). Instead he folded the page and returned it to his pocket. He stopped to listen; had he heard footsteps? The only sound was of the water against the rocks. He descended the hill. Approaching the house he saw his father seated on the steps outside the back door. He sat down on the curb opposite, and waited...

...It seemed that he was standing at the threshold of a long and unpleasant period, marked by increased scrutiny and attention; the thought of the coming weeks and months overwhelmed and exhausted him. He would be systematically denied any access to her, and yet she was the only good thing in his life! He felt a visceral frustration at the injustice of it all. He had only this life, only these brief years! In a few short centuries even the writing of his tombstone would be gone. And yet they spent their time playing this ridiculous and arbitrary game; it was a waste: a fantastic waste! He buried his face in the bundled blanket and wept.

It seemed he could do nothing to make them understand; he was imprisoned by his father's refusal to see or hear him! He felt all the helplessness of the accused who, though innocent, finds himself confronted with his accusers' certainty of his guilt. Any point he raised was received as a pleading excuse (regardless of content, his father heard only an attempt to justify his actions and reduce his punishment!); yes! To his father he remained only an insubordinate child, whose most articulate arguments could be dismissed as nothing more than the pleading of the submitted…

How wholly absurd! It was as though he stood behind a glass partition, expressing the intricacies of his yearning heart while his father, standing beyond, showed in his expression and manner that he heard nothing of what was said. And worse, refused to hear, had no desire to hear! For the partition was of his father's construction: whatever attempts he made were muted against the wall of his father's indifference; what could he do but weep? Nothing: he could do nothing! He opened his mouth to speak; his inability to articulate these revelations overwhelmed him, and he again collapsed into sobs...

# 7

His father rose from the step; there was no need for such vexation! They would talk in the morning. Would his son please come inside? His son rose from the curb and followed his father up the steps to the back door. They said goodnight in the kitchen; Costard's son descended the stairs, lay awake in the dark…

Costard went upstairs, his wife sat up when he came in; what had happened? Costard waved her off; he was too tired to talk now! He would tell her in the morning. She protested; she was very anxious to know! Had he found out where their son went, what he did? She needed to know!

He grew rapidly irritated with her; he had told her that they would talk in the morning! He'd had a very long day, and wanted nothing more than for it to be over! If she wanted to know what was going on with their son, she should go and ask him! He had been sitting outside for two hours; now he wanted to sleep! Was that so much to ask? He had done what she asked him to do! What more did she want from him?

(His wife, smirking, agreed: he was right; he was absolutely right! Fine; it was just fine with her! He did so much; it was unfair for her to ask anything else of him! She supposed it was unfair to ask anything of him! After all: his work was so important; he could not be bothered with such trivial matters! By all means he deserved his rest; by all means he should go to bed!)

Disregarding her he got into bed and closed his eyes. Eventually he relaxed and began to sleep. But soon he awoke suddenly: he'd had a dream in which he was made of wood. He was a bedpost in the bed he shared with his wife, skillfully carved and inlaid with gold and silver. His roots stretched into the ground; he had been carved from the trunk of a still-living tree, and the bed assembled around him! But presently there was a commotion outside the door; the order had been given for the bed to be moved. The door opened and a man came in; he was carrying a handsaw and he knelt and began to cut the post from its roots…

## 8

…Costard had some errands to run; would his son go with him? They would finish their conversation; it was very important to him! (He waited outside while his son dressed; they descended the stairs to the street, began walking…)

His son had to understand: he was still only a child! It was his parents' job to look out for his safety; it was in his best interest! He hoped that one day his son would understand (one day, when his son had children of his own, he would understand!); some mistakes could not be undone, carried consequences that could not be erased with an apology; the world was not a forgiving place!

Could his son appreciate what he was saying? His son shook his head; the street ahead was crowded with people, and his son had not heard the question. Costard yelled to be heard over the noise: he knew that his son was growing up! But it was a dangerous time in a young man's life: a time when one's challenges sometimes got ahead of one's abilities! Did his son understand what he was trying to say?

(They reached the end of the block, a pair of police cars blocked the road, a makeshift barrier had been erected beyond; a half-dozen uniformed officers stood in a line beside the cars and Costard yelled to them: what was going on? One of the officers replied that it was a protest march, that the street would be closed for several hours…)

Costard turned back to his son, but watched instead as his son pushed into the crowd and disappeared between the bodies. Costard called to him, then followed; he made little and slow progress within the dense assembly. He grew rapidly discouraged: certainly he would never locate his son within the crowd! But ahead of him the crowd opened into a ring around a man standing on the hood of a car, shouting into a megaphone. Costard pushed his way to the front and, looking for his son, happened to see instead the girl; she was standing opposite him at the edge of the circle. He started towards her, but paused when another emerged from the crowd beside her; she turned and he watched, unnoticed, as she pulled his face to hers…

(Someone grabbed Costard's arm, he turned back and saw his son…)

## 9

What did he think he was doing? And who did he think he was? And what had they just talked about? Had his son heard a word he'd said? He took his son by the arm and started back in the direction they had come. His son pulled away, jostling several of those standing beside them; he did not want to go! Costard did not care! (Those nearby had noticed them and others were noticing too; a small clearing formed rapidly around them; the man with the megaphone halted his speech;

looking out into the clearing Costard saw that she had noticed them as well...)

# 10

...Walking home Costard attempted several times to speak, but broke off each time, laughing. Eventually his son asked him what was funny. He replied that nothing was funny. Arriving home, he went upstairs and took a shower. He was fine; yes, everything was fine! After all: he was not in love with the girl! He'd had feelings for her - it was only natural that he have feelings for her! - but one always had feelings for anyone that shared one's life! It was only human; one could not help it! But love? The very idea was absurd!

And anyway, he'd known that it could not last! How long had he really expected it to continue? It was always only a matter of time; he knew enough to know that! He was not so naïve as to think that what they had was anything but what it was...

Regardless, wasn't he growing tired of her? Yes; she was far too young for him in a number of ways! It was a relief; yes, it was a relief to be done with her! (And of course these things happened: there were countless instances of the same in literature. He was certain that, if he had a chance to think, he could come up with several examples.)

He finished dressing and left the bathroom, and was surprised to discover his wife standing in the hallway opposite, at the top of the stairs. (For a moment he was overcome: he was certain she had never looked so beautiful; she was the love of his life! He wanted to tell her, to kiss her, to hold her!) As he came forward she moved slightly back. She could not blame him, really! If she was in his shoes, she probably would have done the same. All of those pretty, free-spirited girls, all so enthralled by him, impressed by him: their Professor!

How did he do it? Did he ask them to stay after class? Did he pretend that it was innocent? Did he make them feel special, tell them that he could see in their essays the workings of an artist's sensitive soul? Or did he do it for grades? Or just for fun? He could tell her; she wanted him to tell her! Did they brag about him to their girlfriends? Did it make him feel good? Well did it? He could tell her; she wanted to know! She leaned back against the wall and waited.

## 11

He felt dizzy, and leaned back against the doorframe. But then he laughed: he did not know what she was talking about; she was being ridiculous! He did not know what she thought she knew, but he could assure her that she did not know anything. Yes! Yes, that was it; she did not know anything about his students, or his work, or his life…

His wife shook her head. There'd been a telephone call while he was in the shower. Costard nodded. He could not look at his wife, and so stared at the blank wall opposite. He was filled with an irrepressible hatred for his son; how horrible! Yet he could hardly help himself; it might have been so simple! If his son had simply stayed by his side, the entire episode would never have occurred. And now… He was overwhelmed and exhausted by the thought of the times that lay ahead. The end seemed very far away, and the interval between demanding of such impossible effort. And over so simple a thing! It was almost laughable. He sat down on the floor, leaned his head against the wall, closed his eyes…

## 12

It was strange; it was so strange! A person could live his whole life and yet wake up to find that he did not recognize any of the things he knew: that his world, so long ignored, had become foreign; that he himself had become a foreigner. He had never been unfaithful to her before; she had to believe that! He did not know what to say. He saw her standing at a window, singing; it was so ridiculous! His whole life had suddenly seemed an absurd pageant marching first to the grave and then quickly after into forgotten infinity, resting inconsequentially on nothing whatsoever…

He did not know what to say. If she told him what to say, he would say it. If there was something he could do or say that would make it all right, he would do it. What could he do? What should he do?

She did not want to discuss it while her sister was here. When her sister was gone they would sit down and discuss it. He nodded; yes, whatever she wanted! Whatever she asked him to do he would do...

# 13

They awoke to find that Hermione was gone: the letter she left said only that it had not been an easy decision, and that if they loved her they would not try to find her or stop her. Leontes and his daughter stayed another week, and then took a bus home. A week later, Costard moved into an apartment across town.

What was she going to do? She did not know what she was going to do; she needed some time to think. He left most of his things at the house, and went over to pick up things he needed. After a week of this she asked him to call first; she did not want to be in the house when he was there. After that he decided that he did not need most of the things he had left behind.

He called the girl; would she have dinner with him? He hated that things had ended so badly between them! She hesitated, then agreed; he made reservations and sat waiting for her. She arrived but did not sit: she could not stay; she was sorry about what had happened, but did not think that there was any point in dragging things out! She had only come because she felt that she owed it to him to tell him in person. She would always love him in her own way; she hoped that he knew that!

He did not say anything. She had to be going; she kissed his cheek. She was sure that she would see him around; she wished him the best!

# 14

He went to campus to clean out his office, but stopped at the telephone booth outside to call his wife. Should they get together and talk? It had been almost a month; shouldn't they get together? His wife replied that she was on her way out the door, and did not have time to talk. He grew suddenly annoyed: he did not know why she insisted on doing this! Would she listen to herself, giving him excuses for why she would not talk to him? If she did not want to see him he wished that she would just say it! He laughed. What was she doing, what were they doing? This whole arrangement was absurd: so absolutely absurd!

She was hanging up now; she did not want him calling the house. When she wanted to talk to him, she would call him.

Would she wait? He began to cry. He was sorry; he was sorry he had yelled at her! It was just that he missed her so much; he missed them both so much! He was so miserable without them: so achingly miserable! He turned away from the glass. But all of the walls were glass, and there was no way to stand so that he could not be seen. He covered his face with his hand and wept. It was so frustrating; nothing he said made any difference! She seemed entirely indifferent to his words; a pantomime would have been as effective!

He struck the telephone box with the receiver; he did not care if he was seen! The noise filled the small glass room; his tears were abated by his outburst. He looked around to see if he was observed. The sidewalk and lawn around him were empty; there were no cars in the street…

He lifted the receiver; was she there? Yes, but she really was on her way out. She was going to be late. And besides, she thought it better that she not speak to him: she did not want to say anything she might regret. When she felt ready to talk, she would call him. Until then she would appreciate it if he would not call her.

What was she going to do? She did not know what she was going to do. She'd met with a lawyer; she was making herself aware of her options. He hung up the phone and went inside.

## 15

He sat down behind his desk; had he really spoken to his wife only moments before? How strange! The memory was like that of something imagined, was shrouded in the same mist of impossibility: as though he had dreamed it up and, as a dream, had immediately dismissed it. How odd! He could feel the salt on his cheeks, yet he could not recall what, specifically, had inspired his tears. But of course, in the moment they were shed, he had felt himself fully encumbered and enshrouded by their inspiring circumstance: how strange! For those circumstances now seemed no more substantial than a spider's web blown free of its frame and carried on the empty air, intact… Yes! And soon even this would cease, death would make an end to these meager organic functions: his body would retain the appearance of autonomy long enough to be placed underground, at which point the musculature would release its claim upon the skin, his face would slacken and become unfamiliar, his clothes would decompose in the earth and there would be little left, in time, to indicate who he had been, his familiar face having now returned to anonymous bone…

(He gazed up at his shelves, the titles stared blankly back; how ridiculous he was! His life, his various trials and concerns, enacted within their minor spheres, comprised a laughable farce whose insignificance he had only begun to realize. Had he imagined that some profound revelation lay at the heart of his transgression? How laughable he was: how wholly absurd!

He removed his books from the shelves and loaded them into boxes, then carried the first of these down the hall to the stairwell. Carrying the box before him he could not see the stairs; overestimating the first step his heel struck the second; his ankle turned and he fell forward. He let go of the box to reach out for the railing; the box turned over and the books fell out. His hand missed the railing, he continued falling forward; he struck the stairs and then rolled over. Arriving at the landing his head struck the floor; his body relaxed and he slid and came to a stop against the wall. He groaned and began to rise, but felt dizzy and lay back down. He looked at his books; most of them were still on the stairs, but some had fallen to the landing. Without getting up he gathered the nearest copies into a pile. When he was finished he noticed blood on the tiles under his face. It surprised and confused him. He rolled to his side and tried again to sit up. He was dizzy and there was something else. He could not put his finger on it. He lay back and yawned. He had to get up, but was suddenly so tired! He could not see the harm in resting before he tried again. He closed his eyes and rested.

## 16

He awoke in the hospital; he was aware of someone touching him, but was unable to locate the sensation. There was a mild pressure somewhere in his body. He tried to sit up, but experienced a sharp pain through his stomach and lay back down. A number of hands pressed his arms and shoulders. Someone told him to relax. Someone placed a mask over his mouth and nose. The pain in his stomach subsided and after a moment he closed his eyes and slept.

When he woke up again the room was dark, and a curtain was pulled around his bed. He tried to sit up, but the pain in his stomach again prevented him. A while later he called out: was there someone there who could tell him what was going on? Beyond the drawn curtain someone coughed; there was no other reply…

He was still so very tired! Certainly someone would come and talk to him in the morning; yes, there was nothing to do but wait until morning. He was so unnaturally tired; certainly his questions could wait! He pushed his head back into the pillows and closed his eyes. But he suddenly came fully awake: he did not know what had happened to his books! Had anyone retrieved them? Many of his favorite volumes he had placed in that box; what if someone took them, or some had been lost? He attempted to sit up, but felt again the pain in his stomach and lay back down.

His concern over his books was immediately replaced by this new, more pressing concern; how odd that it had not confronted him earlier, when he first experienced it! But now: what could it mean? He did not know; he did not know! What if something was horribly wrong? (What if they had done all they could, and now could only wait and see? What if they thought he might die in the night? (He imagined, suddenly and clearly, the casket and the flowers, heard the voice of the choir; he saw the mound of dirt and the waiting shovels…) He imagined doctors with reserved faces, shaking their heads and deciding to say nothing, to let him go quietly in his sleep…)

But he wanted to know! If these moments were his last he wanted to know! Even if he could do nothing: even if there was no time in which to make any final, meaningful gesture! Even then he would want to know!

## 17

And all because he happened to pause outside the bookstore and see her standing at the window; how absurd! And now he would die: yes, in this hospital bed his body joined with an eternity of bodies: each room of the hospital held bodies and each building beside the hospital held other bodies and beyond this, the houses and the other towns which also held bodies, and the other countries and finally the world which held millions of bodies, bodies beyond comprehension, bodies walking upon the earth and the bodies that were already beneath the earth, bodies that inhaled and exhaled gasses, bodies that grew big and gave birth and bodies whose mechanisms failed, bodies that ceased to circulate blood and ceased to draw in breath and his was only one of them; how absurd! His body and the bodies of all those living in his time would cease and rot and disappear; yes, the world was an odd collection of corpses, a production of corpses, a parade of corpses, a mass and unmarked grave!

He tried to roll over in bed, the pain in his stomach prevented him; how he loathed his body! (His pathetic body, his prison!) He would not be denied the comfort of pressing his face into the pillow, of blocking out the vision of the drawn curtain, the darkened room! He persevered and succeeded in turning to his hip. Something else now prevented him; he could not move his leg. He attempted to bend his knee; his knee would not move. He wiggled his toes. He thought they responded, but in the dark he could not be sure. Reaching out and down along his body, he felt the near edge of the thick plaster cast that ringed his upper thigh.

The strain of reaching was too much; he fell back against the sheets. The pain in his stomach did not subside for several minutes. He could not stand it! Overcome with self-pity, he sobbed into his open palms. His moans echoed inside his hands; a voice from beyond the curtain called for quiet. Surprised, he forgot the pain in his stomach. He lay still, feeling embarrassed for crying and feeling foolish for having disturbed whomever was beyond the curtain. When he remembered the pain in his stomach it had significantly subsided.

## 18

His former thoughts seemed strange to him: had he really imagined (only moments before!) that the world comprised only a mass and unmarked grave? How odd! He remembered the idea exactly, yet could not recall what, specifically, had inspired that conclusion. He wondered again if anyone had gathered together his books: they were some of his most cherished volumes! He hoped that none had been damaged in the fall; he hoped that none had been lost! And had anyone called his wife? Someone must have; the family was always notified. (Yes: very likely she had stood beside him through the time that he could not remember, between the fall and the moment he awoke, feeling unseen hands upon him...)

Yes, his wife; how he longed to see her, to be near her! She and their son were his whole world; he could not live without them, did not want to live without them; how he loved them! Sunday laundry, the weekly rotation of dinners, the customary quiet in the hour before bed, the litany of familiar conversations, the alternate mornings driving their son to school: how pleasant the familiar structure of his former life had been! And now, how cruelly denied: what horror, that those (once-loathed) hours could not now be reclaimed! He wished only to return; he wished only to return!

How pleasant it was! Vaguely considered, his former life seemed a wonder whose honeyed promises devalued all that he had once imagined lay beyond. Had he imagined that the girl would make him happy? How ridiculous that belief now seemed: how laughable and naïve! (Yes: and he himself was laughable for having believed it; he was a fool: undeniably a fool!)

He felt exceedingly tired. Descending into sleep he became irrationally convinced that his wife would arrive at any moment. Certainly she would: the family was always notified! She would see him and understand his regret (would see how minor was his transgression, when weighed against the bulwark of their life together!); soon she would help him rise, and lead him home… How pleasant the coming years would be! Beneath her perpetual gaze his sins would soon lose their consequence, their life would continue on; one would lead the other until both fell from life. And then their trials and vexations would be washed away by a blank and blessed forgetfulness...

How pleasant it would be; how he loved her! How he had always loved her!

# CANTO TWELVE § "THE ACCOLADES I HEAPED UPON MYSELF WERE MADE WORTHLESS BY THE LOWNESS OF THEIR PROFESSOR…"

# 1

(Faithful companion: have you traveled this far? I applaud and humbly thank you!)

No more remains, no passage awaits (no passage in which I may yet achieve that which I have failed to grasp!); ignoble and worldly these poor players have scratched their progress in the banal realm beneath heaven and come to nothing! (Yes; and you see now final - irrefutable! – proof of my meager talents! Know that I share your very thoughts!)

Yet it comes now to little consequence: my previous concerns stand as woefully laughable in light of those strange events that followed quickly on the heels of my Cordelia's last-mentioned praise. (Yes, and all fictions equally laughable: my childish impulse and impetus revealed (my never-ending pursuit of that ethereal maternal regard!) I can only relegate these efforts to their appropriate sphere and declare them that which is to be overcome before a life might be enacted; O, my ridiculous refusals and guileless dodges! How the Devil within me laughs!)

(But I am almost finished: there is little left to tell! May I implore you further? Will you travel these few remaining pages with me? Faithful companion I thank you! Do you recall my Cordelia's blank ambivalence, or have you forgotten her already? Faithful companion I envy you, wish that I might do the same…)

Recall that bitter basking in Cordelia's indifference I rambling rendered clown Claudio, that she praised him above all others, that I was overjoyed (returned, like a lover scorned, to supplicate myself before the necessity of her praise…); my Cordelia had applauded my efforts, there seemed no other test; this too faded! I soon again found myself hounded by doubt, haunted by recriminations and self-accusations of deficiency and failure, and I longed again for her substantiation: her slightest kind word seemed sufficient to validate all my hours of revision and reversal (hours I felt myself always in danger of discovering as worthless, wasted, lost)! I could not bear it, I begged her to meet me, at our accustomed place…

I arrived first, in a great excitement and anxious for her arrival. My thoughts since had been clear and (strangely, easily!) articulate: in the course of five days I had reviewed and rewritten dozens of pages; I worked in a frenzy and with a self-assurance I had previously found only rarely, and often not at all. (These pages I kept in an envelope inside my coat, secured close to my skin: I felt them there with each breath; they were, in that moment, more precious than life!) When she arrived I waved her over; she saw me, but stopped first to order from the barman. I sat at the table in miserable self-doubt: was I to go to her at the bar? Did she expect me to wait at the table? (There seemed little danger that, were I to go to her, the table would be occupied when we returned: the bar was nearly empty, and from the hour one could guess that few other patrons would arrive.) I decided, regardless to wait; I removed the envelope from the coat pocket and placed it before one of the empty places. (I will admit that my heart raced, anticipating her praise! Never had I more clearly articulated the profound; never had my words more dexterously grasped the ether!)

I was thus thrown into confusion when, arriving (and, I had no doubt, perceiving the envelope's contents and request), she seated herself at one of the other places (how clearly I remember it: the envelope, offered to a vacancy!). I kissed her cheek, her skin was cold; undeterred I expressed my great joy: my thoughts had been clear and lucid; my words had never more ably grasped the Olympian ether to which they aspired! Perceiving her foul humor I expressed my certainty that it was she who was responsible, to whom I owed my thanks! This flattery did nothing to alter her state or earn her acknowledgment, I did not know what else to say; I sat back in my seat, despairing at the pleasant evening which now seemed lost, and the praise which she seemed unwilling to give…

The envelope, still facing the empty place, now inspired contempt within me: doubtless it was the presence of the envelope that had caused her ill humor! Certainly she had no wish to be burdened with my ridiculous ramblings, my so-called Art! Who was I, to make these demands? A simpleton, a fool! (In light of accusations the contents of my envelope seemed ridiculous, paltry: truly one so base as myself could produce nothing so lofty as that which I had congratulated myself for having done; the accolades I heaped upon myself were made worthless by the lowness of their professor!)

## 2

(What divine (what final, what absolute!) authority I ascribed to my Cordelia! Her lightest word was sufficient to send me to the heights of Heaven or the depths of Hell; such was my state! Wracked and nervous, prone to delirium, frantic with passion one moment and becalmed by despair in the next! And with what justification: that I aspired to the Apollic ideals, that I fancied myself the Gods' poet? What a low being I have since discovered myself to be! For I have since entertained sordid fantasies, committed bestial acts, indulged in the brutish stupor, have (in short) given myself over to that life which concerns itself always and only with the distance between plate and mouth, have abandoned all higher aspiration and succumbed to the calling of that eternal emptiness whose passage leads through life's lowest refuse but which, finally, has no bottom…)

I drank without tasting, I looked without seeing: my sore travail and sorrow (my doubt and frustration, my failure!) condensed to the singular point of the worthless envelope (in which I had gathered all of my hope and faith; for which, moments before, I had hoped to gain transcendent affirmation and absolution!). How ridiculous I was: how laughable!

## 3

My Cordelia sitting opposite seemed more distant than a lost paradise (a distance across which her previous praise whispered echoing mockery!); convinced that the encounter was past redemption, I resolved to take my leave of her. But as I stood (I even offered some excuse: so highly did I regard her that I felt moved to explain myself!) she spoke: she was bored with this place! I, too startled to continue on my intended course, offered that I had assumed (since I had first met her here, that rain-soaked night some weeks before!) that she frequented the establishment of her own volition. She corrected me: not at all! She'd simply been caught out in the rain and, having no desire to combat the elements, had ducked inside to wait out the ensuing storm.

(Did this base explanation dissipate whatever fantastical elements still swirled in my memory of that night? Did this reasonable story reveal as ridiculous my private rendering of her as my angel, my temptress, my muse? Not at all: so ready was I to again embrace her in my heart (to love her as one loves one's God!) that I saw in her story the workings of divine serendipity: a subtle hand moved the pieces of fate; it was no chance that she was walking by, when the clouds chanced to open!)

Where would she rather go? (Had the earth opened and she descended into hell's burning depths, I would not have hesitated to follow!) She knew of a place, it was not far; I hurriedly settled our bill and followed her out into the street. The night was warm with no threat of clouds, she put her arm through mine (the envelope, since returned to my pocket, pressed into my skin); we descended a stair into a swale and walked along the river; the cooler air atop the water showed our breath. Merry lights showed on the banks above; we walked until even the last of these had disappeared into the trees. Finally I perceived a mount of rocks shoring up the crumbling bank ahead; we climbed this and stood on the edge of a broad flat expanse. In the center stood a tin-roofed shack emanating light and music (I marveled at how completely it was obscured by trees and the noise from the rushing waters; had we not climbed the rocks I might never have noticed it); we approached, Cordelia knocked; the door was opened and we were ushered inside...

## 4

What a fantastic sight! We stood upon a short stair leading down to the cabin's dugout floor and from atop which we could see over the heads of the horde packed inside. A makeshift bar stood against the cabin's opposite wall whereat a mountainous bartender conversed with a slender stalk of a man, himself busily engaged in sorting through records while the culprit of the pervading noise spun round on the table before him. Between these and ourselves there was no floor visible: having little room to move themselves the poor souls seemed content to move in a kind of unnatural unison (I remembered returning to an overripe piece of fruit left too long on the vine only to find it now pulsing with an abhorrent collection of writhing white maggots; I was certain, in my ignorant youth, that such were the protruding tentacles of some horrid creature, whose upper portion was wholly engaged and obscured within the fruit's interior; standing atop the stair it seemed I beheld the same again!)

Yet the stern voice of the doorman returned me to myself; what were we waiting for? Did we intend to stand in the doorway all night? My Cordelia took my hand, we descended the stair; the cooling draft by the door quickly became only a distant memory in the face of the sickening heat which rose from the many bodies and, having no escape, fell back down upon them. I feared that I would sweat through my shirt, and so ruin the contents of my envelope. I had no time, however, to protest; my Cordelia pulled me deeper into the room (I was surprised: from above the room seemed not much larger than my own garret and yet within the crowd seemed to stretch on and on, the far wall to retreat into the distance…). Finally we arrived at the bar, the barman turned to us; recognizing Cordelia, he kissed her cheek; the slender man (glancing up from his records) did the same; she returned both and ordered drinks whose name I failed to hear over the clamor behind and around us…

The barman mixed them expertly, the slender man placed a new record beneath the needle (the noise hardly abated in this pause, so boisterous was the crowd); our drinks were placed before us, she touched her glass to mine. We drank down the barman's concoction; it was sweet on the tongue and fire in the chest, and I was immediately overcome as by a potion. Cordelia asked (with gestures) for my verdict; I replied (with gestures) my enthusiastic endorsement; she ordered (with gestures) two more. I resolved to watch carefully the procedure, but found my thoughts wandering; I felt a kind of playful indifference, a nonchalance and blitheness absent from my constitution since earliest childhood. The barman set the glasses before us, she again touched hers to mine; again we drank and again I tasted the sweetness and felt the fire. She took my hand, we entered the crowd; I do not know for how long we danced, only that when we again retreated to the meager haven of the bar my clothes were soaked through and I felt wholly indifferent to the ruined pages still held tight against me within my coat…

(The room seemed then a warm embrace, a bastion, a womb: I entertained fantasies that I would linger there forever, drinking the barman's curious potion and basking in my Cordelia's (now benevolent!) gaze…)

## 5

Of course it was not to last! The song ended and before the slender man had a chance to replace it I heard someone calling my Cordelia's name; a man emerged from the crowd; is it not redundant to relate the circumstances that followed? I myself have grown so weary of thinking of them… (No: I must! For I am haunted still by the expression she wore when she turned and saw him, with what joy she threw herself into his arms, pressed her lips to his… Would that I could cast that memory from me!

And how my fortress changed: the room's warm embrace became a smothering hold, became prison bars, became Satan's teeth!)

I have little recollection of what followed, only of running along the river for what seemed like hours: I stumbled as I descended the rocks, and fell; jagged edges scraped my palms and the mud and water at the bottom chilled me. I hoped at every turn to perceive again those merry lights on the banks above me, but each turn brought only trees and darkness; there was not even a moon with which to find my way! Eventually I located the stairs (I reasoned, later, that it was by that time late, and the lights had all been extinguished); I climbed the hill and located my door; I collapsed inside into drunken and fevered dreams...

What had occurred? I had barely any recollection, I could not be certain: for a time I was convinced that I had struck the man; in another dream it seemed that I had lunged at him with a fragment of broken glass, but had missed and struck my Cordelia in the throat; in yet another I saw the assembly turning cruel faces to laugh as I pushed between them to flee. For two days I lay in agonies, barely rising from the floor as the fever ran its course, hardly able to tell dream from truth (at one point I saw my Cordelia bending attentively over me; at other moments I felt phantom blows, as of the man's boots in my side…); eventually I was able to rise and prepare some meager repast; some time later my faculties returned to me, and these events seemed, in their totality, to constitute a strange hallucination, a delirium from which I was only now emerging. Still, the cuts on my palms (from where I had tumbled down the rocky embankment) could not be denied…

I had no idea what I had done, and spent the next week half-expecting policemen to arrive and haul me away for some vaguely remembered assault or murder. Was it possible that I had struck my Cordelia? I did not know! My memories seemed incredible…

But the police did not come, and soon I began to feel sheepish and ashamed: certainly nothing had occurred; my violent dreams were only that; I was guilty of nothing worse than acting like a fool (the memory of cruel faces turning to laugh - even if a fantasy! - was never distant from my thoughts)!

(This feeling was tempered by a separate sensation, growing as the other dissipated, which came to the forefront of my psychic life as the other retreated into memory: I was overcome with an oppressive loneliness, a sorrow that my ridiculous behavior (my frantic retreat) now barred me from my Cordelia. I could not face her, a fact made all the more sorrowful by my having long since become accustomed to thinking fondly of her, to retreating into pleasant fantasies. Thus my imagination mocked me; I felt torn apart at the quarters, dismantled in many directions by black memory and sinister passions which seemed at every moment eager to shatter my ever-more fragile state…)

## 6

Finally my loneliness overwhelmed my shame: I returned to the place where she had first appeared to me (her hair wet from the rain, her dress clinging to her skin): I would wait until she returned; I would sit until the clouds chose to open, until she was caught again in unexpected downpour… What Gods there were would not deny me one more vision!

I left the bar that evening crestfallen but undaunted, more resolute in my desire. If I was required to thus repent, to spend my hours in purgatory before being once again granted admittance to her angelic presence, so be it! I felt certain that my efforts occurred under the watchful eye of some ethereal jury, that my lonely walk home did not go unacknowledged!

Such madness! It seems obvious now (what at first was only a passing suspicion now seems immutable, shouts with the resounding knell of truth!) that no Cordelia ever sat down beside me, her hair wet and dripping and her dress clinging to her ankles: that fragments of the real and the true blended into dreams to form delusions whose mendacity my overworked brain failed to perceive. This fantastical explanation astounds me with its cool logic, shines like a winter's sunbeam through the gray fog of my turbulent interior. When I feel the madness returning I have only to ask the doctors to tell the story, and then it is again clear (that I felt myself failing to climb to those lofty and intangible ethereal heights, and that in my self-loathing, my shame and disappointment I invented one to hold above me, to guide and comfort me, to be my savior and my muse...)

Yes; she was my girl singing behind glass, my Beatrice, my Siren calling me to ripe wisdom and quickened spirit (when I hear this explanation I am released, I feel absolved, I weep with gratitude)...

For it was irrefutable evidence that brought me here; if ever I begin to doubt (if I dream, and in my dream imagine that she is singing to me beyond my prison walls) I need only recall that in final desperation I descended the stairs to the cool riverbed (I had since perceived that no jury on high observed my lonely and nightly walk home!), that I walked through mud and brambles until I came upon that mount of rocks, that I summited and perceived the cabin, that I was met on my approach by an old man who, exiting the property, demanded to know my business there, that, so frantic was I, I pushed past him and entered, that (no doubt you have already guessed!) the cabin was much changed from my memory, that it displayed no bar or sunken floor, that a small woodstove stood in the corner, that its floorboards and furniture showed a thick coat of dust, disturbed in places as by the movements of a single occupant of unchanging habits and lengthy residence...

And yet (it is with horror that I recall) I was not satisfied: I took the old man by the collars and demanded to know what was meant by this subterfuge, by this absurd and vast orchestration. He struck me, he clawed at my cheeks (so impassioned was I that I did not feel their sting!); we fell to the floor and I, perceiving that the fireplace iron was near, took and raised it; I let fly, his bare scalp (his face was turned away, crawling, as he was, upon his stomach) collapsed...

What followed (I scoured the floor boards for an entrance to the space I felt breathing below; finding it, I descended and found a root cellar whose various and worn ornaments bespoke decades of sedentary neglect) remains with me as the memory of a fevered dream; I left him where he lay and made the long return. I thought that perhaps it had been a dream (the cabin, after all, had been so different from what I knew it to be!), I made my mind busy with other thoughts. Yet there were scratches on my cheeks; I could not deny my sin (I felt still the trembling iron in my hands, the horrible and surprising fatigue that followed: as though by taking his life I had nearly exhausted my own)! I did not leave my apartment for seven days, I awaited the falling hammer...

## 7

But no police came, and I was left to the punishing demons of my own conscience and speculation. Perhaps the crime had not been discovered; perhaps the body had been dragged away by some beast, whose hunger (when the old man's disappearance was brought to light) would be blamed. Perhaps the old man had neither family nor visitors; certainly the cabin was secluded, would not be found by idle pedestrians. Nor would they likely approach (I had been certain to close the door behind me; the cabin would look as though occupied, self-contained, bloodless!); I began to feel that perhaps the crime would go uninvestigated, that my transgression might escape discovery…

Yet I was haunted, wracked, beset by nerves; I saw at every turn the old man's wide-eyed terror, heard his frantic cries (yes, visions of my Cordelia had been entirely replaced by immutable memory; I could not escape the enclosed prison of my own ever-circling thoughts!); in short, I felt myself succumbing to madness; my family (as you have no doubt inferred) is of some means, and following a brief consultation with a panel of doctors (familiars from mother's parties and father's meetings) it was agreed that I sequester here until I am deemed sufficiently recovered.

(Here in the restful bosom of manicured garden paths and white linen I feel finally pervasive peace, am haunted neither by dreams nor aspirations, have become like the timeless angels lingering in changeless heaven…)

But now I have made my confession; yes! They will read these notes, these pages and by them find his body or what skeleton remains (will perceive the crumpled skull, now exposed, the iron sitting still handily by!); yes! No defense will stand in the face of such evidence and confession: a declaration of insanity will not stand against my eloquence, my obvious intelligence, my commendable faculties! (No: the jury will see that I am too clever to be called incompetent: yes they will see and punish accordingly!) Nor have I any reason to attempt escape, it is death I seek: yes, death and this forever angelic peace, this white linen cloud, this blessed flight and absolution!

The gas chamber awaits: I see it before me! The vapors rise and enfold me, I drift to blessed dissolution… No, do not weep for me, for I die an Artist! My poor cast enacting their worthless escapades upon a barren stage before an empty house stands: my monument to the unattainable, the inarticulate and ethereal! Nothing else survives; nothing more remains!

But now I hear her calling; she is just beyond my prison walls! I will finish here and relinquish these pages to her: perhaps some guard will find them! Yes: he does the work of Law; I cannot lament that through his brutish hands my shattered life will be delivered, rendered forth…

How absurd that he has become my savior! How I weep with gratitude!

## About The Author

Stavros Stavros lives and works in Cleveland, Ohio.

He is the author of everything you will find at StavrosStavros.Blogspot.Com.

*The Sirens* is his first novel.

www.ingramcontent.com/pod-product-compliance
Lightning Source LLC
Chambersburg PA
CBHW030305180626
46810CB00003B/923